BEN AND THE SUDDEN *TOO-BIG!* FAMILY

By **Colby Rodowsky**

What About Me?
Evy-Ivy-Over
P.S. Write Soon
A Summer's Worth of Shame
The Gathering Room
H, My Name Is Henley
Keeping Time
Julie's Daughter
Fitchett's Folly
Sydney, Herself
Dog Days
Jenny and the Grand Old Great-Aunts
Lucy Peale
Hannah In Between
Sydney, Invincible
Remembering Mog
The Turnabout Shop
Not My Dog
Spindrift
Clay
Jason Rat-a-tat
Not Quite a Stranger
The Next-Door Dogs
That Fernhill Summer

BEN AND THE SUDDEN TOO-BIG! FAMILY

COLBY RODOWSKY

FARRAR STRAUS GIROUX

NEW YORK

Copyright © 2007 by Colby Rodowsky
Distributed in Canada by Douglas & McIntyre Ltd.
Printed in the United States of America
Designed by Barbara Grzeslo
First edition, 2007
1   3   5   7   9   10   8   6   4   2

www.fsgkidsbooks.com

Library of Congress Cataloging-in-Publication Data
Rodowsky, Colby F.
    Ben and the sudden too-big family / Colby Rodowsky.— 1st ed.
        p.   cm.
    Summary: Until now, ten-year-old Ben has believed that life is
made up of "all right" and "not all right" stuff, but when his
father remarries and the couple adopts a Chinese baby, he
wonders which kind of stuff will prevail.
    ISBN-13: 978-0-374-30658-8
    ISBN-10: 0-374-30658-3
    [1. Family life—Fiction.   2. Adoption—Fiction.]   I. Ben
and the sudden too big family.   II. Title.

PZ7.R6185 Ben 2007
[Fic]—dc22

                                                    2006044510

With thanks to my family for a wonderful week,
this book is for

Larry,
Laurie and Andres,
Alice and Jimmy,
Emily and Jay,
Sarah and Til,
Julie and Greg,
Kate and Steven

and for the grandchildren,
Andrew,
Maggie,
Katie,
Pilar,
Matthew,
Ryan,
Elizabeth,
Will,
Margaret,
Ellen,
Pedro,
Virginia,
Anna,
Frances

Contents

BEN AND THE SUDDEN TOO-BIG! FAMILY

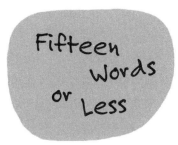

Fifteen Words or Less

It was in the just-after-the-holiday-break part of fourth grade when Mr. Kelly, our English teacher, told us to write our philosophy of life in fifteen words or less. I thought for a minute and then wrote, "Some things in life are all right and some things are not all right." After that, I sat curling and uncurling the edge of my paper and wondering what I should have done with the extra word.

When everyone was finished, Mr. K. folded his arms, harrumphed a bit, the way he always does, and said, "Now elaborate on what you've written."

This led me to add, "What actually happens a lot is that the all-right stuff slides into the not-all-right stuff and what you end up with is a hodgepodge glop. And that's life."

By this time Mr. K. was walking up and down the aisle, looking over our shoulders, and when he got to me he said, "Pretty basic, Ben. Wouldn't you say?" Only I could tell right off that it was one of those questions that wasn't really a question and didn't need an answer. Then he snorted and moved on.

I always figured that that whole philosophy-of-life thing wasn't so much a real assignment as it was a way for Mr. Kelly to kill some dead time on a winter Friday afternoon. I mean, even though he collected our papers, we never got marks or comments, never had to turn them into essays or projects of any kind. If you ask me, it was a good fifteen words or less, plus elaboration, down the drain.

Oddly enough, though, those fourteen words attached themselves to the inside of my head like a refrigerator magnet, and from then on I set out to check everything that happened to me to see if it belonged in the all-right column or not-all-right column. The trouble was, I didn't exactly keep up with the sorting—all right, not all right—mostly, I guess, because during the next year and a half a lot went on in my life.

My name is Benjamin David Mitchell. My father is Mitch, making him Mitch Mitchell, except to people who don't know him well and then he's Bradley J. Mitchell. I'm told that when I was born (ten years before Mr. Kelly's down-the-drain assignment) my mother, Sara Jane, announced that there would be no shortcuts and I would forever be Benjamin David.

Then she died, in a car crash, when I was just over a year old, and left me with lots of pictures but no real memory of a mother. In fact, as far as I can remember, it's always just been me and my dad—Ben and Mitch—which, to my way of thinking, and maybe because I didn't know anything else, made for a pretty cool arrangement. So cool that in my entire life, ten years and counting, the all-right stuff had always been miles out in front of the not-all-right.

The first thing to know about my father is that he has taught history at MacCauley, a private boys' school in Baltimore, for absolute ages. Because of that, I get to go there for free, as a sort of perk or something. The only drawback is that I can never just go home and hang out after school. Instead I have to stick around—in the library or the locker room, or outside playing sports or watching the high school kids at football or lacrosse practice—till my father's ready to leave. After that, we head home together, fix supper, do homework, watch TV, play video games or read (Mitch way more than me), and go to bed. Weekends are pretty much the same, especially since MacCauley is the kind of school where a lot of stuff happens then. Like games and meets, fall fairs and spring fairs, shows and debates, and even car washes. And the dreaded Science Competition.

I guess I'd have to say that good old MacCauley has always been the center of our universe, which isn't nearly as lame as it sounds. I mean, we have a lot of neighbors, too, and get together with them for cookouts and crab feasts and New Year's celebrations. We lend them ladders and snow shovels, and we borrow rakes and duct tape from them, so it all works really well.

And in the family department we have Aunt Jo and Uncle Charlie and their two sons. Scott and Stan are eighteen and nineteen, so not exactly the kind of cousins I can hang out with, but through the years they've been really okay, plus they've given me a bunch of outgrown stuff—like bikes and sleds and skateboards. Besides, their house was where we went for all the heavy-duty celebrating, like Thanksgiving and Christmas, Mitch's birthday, and mine, too. Aunt Jo is Mitch's older (and only) sister and she has this mother-hen thing, always checking to see if we eat enough broccoli and go to the dentist twice a year.

She was also the one who, ages back, introduced my father to my mother and, if you ask me, I think Aunt Jo had thoughts about doing something like that again. For a while now she's been on a mission to "find someone for Mitch" and there's been a steady parade of lawyers, paralegals, librarians, teachers, and even a poet. There've been blondes, brunettes, and three redheads. Sometimes Mitch would ask them out a time or two. Sometimes not. But he was never really interested.

Until the day, not long after Mr. Kelly's assignment, that we stopped at the Bread Basket.

The Bread Basket

You know how some days stick out in your mind and others just go along and eventually lump together? Well, the Bread Basket day was an all-time sticker-outer.

Mitch and I were on our way home from school with nothing much to look forward to but his leftover vegetable stew (heavy on the okra) from the night before. We'd just dropped a movie off at Blockbuster and turned onto Falls Road when Mitch screeched the car over to the curb and said, "Well, will you look at that."

"That what?" I said, hardly glancing up from my science test, where I'd been trying to figure out why Mrs. Savopoulos had given me a B– instead of the A that, in my wildest dreams, I was sure I deserved.

"*That* that. How can you *miss* it?"

And then I saw it—this egg-yolk-yellow house with green trim all around and pots of funky fake flowers out in front. "Where'd that come from?" I asked. "It wasn't there before."

"Yeah, it probably was," said Mitch. "I seem to remember some ramshackly frame house of no particular color. We just never really noticed it, I guess."

"Yeah—so?" I said, turning the science test upside down to see if the B– turned into an A that way.

"Look at the sign. Read it," my father said.

"The Bread Basket," I read out loud.

>"Breads, Rolls, Sweets,
>and Enticements
>C. Coleman
>D. Lynam
>Props."

I stared at the sign a while longer before asking, "What're 'Enticements'? And what're 'Props.'?"

" 'Props.' are proprietors, owners, and let's go in and see what 'Enticements' are," said Mitch, already halfway out of the car. "We've got that leftover stew for supper and could use a loaf of good bread."

And from that day on, we ate a lot more bread than ever before. Also rolls and sweets. "Enticements" turned out to be giftie kinds of things—spicy-smelling tins of teas that weren't your basic Liptons, little boxes of chocolates and packs of wafers, even teapots and dish-drying towels. Stuff. Certainly nothing I'd ever have thought Mitch would've cared about, except that the first time we went into the Bread Basket we met C. Coleman, Prop. Casey.

And, as I said, we were suddenly into bread. But we

didn't just grab a loaf and go either, the way we would've at 7-Eleven or Super Fresh. Each time we went in, we took to lingering while Mitch talked to Casey. In the beginning it was all about bread, but then they got into the Orioles, the latest movie at the Senator or the Charles, and P. D. James mysteries. They even had a conversation about the proper way to visit a museum and whether, at the Smithsonian in Washington, D.C., it was better to spend all your time in one building or to hop around from place to place, seeing little bits of lots of things.

For example, Mitch would say, in his firmest history-teacher voice, "With the Smithsonian, the thing that counts is an early start. You've got to be over in Washington by the time the doors open so you can dig in. You've got to spend the whole day in one museum—American History or Natural History or whatever—but the point is, you have to hunker down and just breathe it all in. And even then, one day doesn't begin to do it . . ." He stopped and shrugged his shoulders. "Now, if you could manage to come back the next day, and the next—same place— maybe in six months or so you'd begin to make a dent."

Then Casey would say, "Oh, nooooo. Too intense. I'm more a bit-of-this-and-a-dab-of-that kind of museum visitor. A couple of hours at Air and Space, a stop at the Hirshhorn, a tour of the sculpture garden, and plenty of time for lunch." Then she'd look over to where I was playing on the floor with her cat, Half-a-Loaf, and wink.

Eventually these conversations led to the three of us

going to a movie at the Senator or the Charles, or down to the harbor, and once even to the Smithsonian, where Casey and I took the hop-around approach, with time out for lunch, and Mitch buried himself in Natural History till it was time to go home.

We did things together like that for a couple of months or so, and—duh—for a while I thought that was the way it was supposed to be. Mitch, Casey, and Ben. Then one night at a baseball game, just after opening day, I looked over from watching the O's manager and the umpire going at it, and saw my father holding Casey's hand and sort of stroking her fingers. Double-duh. *There's something going on here*, I thought in my best genius mode.

Anyway, that's when Aunt Jo and I put our heads together, and the next time (and the one after that, and the one after that, and so on) Mitch mentioned something for the three of us to do, I was suddenly busy. In fact, from then on, I spent a lot more time with Aunt Jo and Uncle Charlie, which they said was all to the good on account of, with Stan away at college and Scott busy with senior-year stuff, their house had been much too quiet lately. And as for me, I got to play a ton more video games than I would have at home and I got to watch a pile of movies. It was all part of my great disappearing-third-person act.

Casey

I don't actually know how long this kind of thing usually takes—the going out and all, I mean. But if you ask me, it was pretty quick from when Aunt Jo and I decided to, as she put it, "give Mitch and Casey some time to themselves" to when my father settled down for a talk one night.

I was at the kitchen table studying for my science exam, which was the next day and seemed to be looming over me like a giant volcano about to erupt, when Mitch pulled out a chair and sat across from me, saying, "Well, Ben, I'd like for the two of us to have a talk."

Right away there were a couple of things wrong with that whole scenario. One was that, to my father's way of thinking, there was nothing more important than *studying for an exam*, and I'm pretty sure that even if the house was on fire he'd think twice about disturbing me to mention it. And two was that, since when did Mitch ever announce that he and I were having a talk? Up to now, if he had something to say, he just said it. No big deal.

"About what?" I said, closing my science book on my

finger and trying to remember how many essay questions Mrs. Savopoulos had said were going to be on the exam and how many were going to be the fill-in-the-blank kind.

"Yes, uh, well, uh, I thought maybe it was time for us to . . . well, you know . . . there's something . . ." My-father-the-articulate-one, the former debate champion, seemed to be drowning in words right before my eyes.

"Yeah?" And even as I asked the question I was flipping through things in my head, trying to figure what kind of trouble I might be in. I mean, as far as I could remember, it'd been a while since any teacher had threatened to "talk to your father, young man." My room wasn't in any worse shape than usual, and I was pretty sure I'd put the recycling stuff out the night before last.

"Yes. Well. I was thinking . . . We were thinking . . ." He stopped, took a deep breath, stared at the clock on the microwave, and then said, "How would it be if I married Casey?"

Married Casey. The words shot through my head like lightning bolts.

"If you married Casey?" I echoed. "It'd be cool."

"I thought you'd feel that way," said Mitch, letting out a giant sigh. "I'm glad you do. And you know, Ben, it'll just be—"

"But, hey, we'll still live *here*, won't we? In this house?" I suddenly asked.

"Of course we will. Casey knows this is your home. *Our* home. Anyway, she'll give up her apartment and she and Half-a-Loaf will move in with us. We'll probably want to do a few things around the house and . . ."

I yanked my finger out of my science book, totally losing my place, and sat back, only half listening to my father as he went on about fresh paint and our having to work at putting the toilet seat down and how, no matter what, the bread would be better. And all the while he was talking, I was thinking about Casey. About how she was tall, with freckles, and hair the color of straw and sun, and how she mostly wore jeans and T-shirts and, when she was at the Bread Basket, a giant white apron. I thought about how she had seen all the *Lord of the Rings* movies a bunch of times over, the same as I had, and had even read the books. Which I hadn't quite gotten to yet. And how she liked the Orioles and didn't like the Yankees, mostly because they *were* the Yankees, and knew that the best parts of ice hockey games were the fights.

I nodded and said, "Yeah, definitely cool."

". . . Of course, bound to be changes. There always are," said Mitch, in a finishing-up way that gave me the clue that maybe I'd missed something. Maybe something important.

"Changes? What kind of changes? I thought you said—the house and all—something about a little paint and well, yeah, the toilet seat."

"The house'll be fine, and Casey will move in, the way I said." But then my-father-the-history-teacher took over. "Change is inevitable. Life evolves. And as we go along, we have to adapt, to adjust, because in the normal progression things shift and, well, change."

"How?" I asked. "Change how?"

"Okay, look at it this way. For a lot of years there've been just the two of us, Ben. Now there'll be three, and maybe someday four," he said.

"Four? Half-a-Loaf won't be a problem," I said.

My father stood up, walked around the table, and then sat down again, leaning in to face me. "Not the *cat*," he said. "I'm talking about another child."

"Another *child*? What child? Casey doesn't have a kid."

"No," said Dad. "But she's always wanted one. Before we even met, she had made plans to adopt a child from China. And now we're weighing the options, trying to decide whether to go ahead with the plans. Somewhere down the road."

"Down the road," I said, and right away that fourth person—that kid—was safely lumped in with all the other down-the-road things in my life, like high school and driving a car and staying up all night on New Year's Eve. "Yeah. Okay, and like I said, that'll be cool."

Just at that moment, tomorrow's science exam seemed a lot more important and a lot more looming, and I reached for my textbook, flipping the pages until I found my place.

• • •

And so we had a wedding. It took place at the courthouse downtown on a Thursday afternoon and was, as Casey described it, one step up from an elopement.

"I know a bunch of people in my family aren't going to like this," she had told me when I'd been hanging out at the Bread Basket one day the week before. "But with different ones living in North Carolina and Pennsylvania and Delaware and even Connecticut—well, this will just be easier. Besides, your dad and I want to keep it small. And intimate. Believe me, Ben, my family can be a little overwhelming all at once."

I'd never actually been to a wedding before, but this one definitely seemed okay. Aunt Jo and Uncle Charlie were there, and Nanny and Fred, too. They were Casey's parents, and I knew from the times I'd already met them that they were really nice. D. Lynam, Prop. (Debbie, the other owner of the Bread Basket), and her husband were there, too, on account of Debbie was the best lady or whatever you call it. And three of the teachers from school, because my father said he couldn't *not* invite them.

Then, at the very last minute, Casey's sister Lois rushed in saying, "I just hopped on a train in Philadelphia and came down for the wedding." With that, she swooped around the room kissing everyone in sight—except me because I hid behind my father.

And speaking of me, I was the best man and got to stand up front next to Mitch and hand him the ring when the time came.

Afterward, we had dinner in Little Italy, and when it was over Mitch and Casey went to New York for a long weekend. I went home with Aunt Jo and Uncle Charlie, and that night I dreamed about bread and a blurry mob of relatives being doled out on a spoon and what it'd be like to have Casey and Half-a-Loaf living with us. I woke up feeling glad from the inside out and thought how maybe Mitch was wrong and things weren't *really* going to change all that much.

That Chinese Baby

Casey moved into our house. She brought some stuff: chairs, dishes that had once belonged to her grandmother, a really old chest, and a zillion books. She and Mitch painted what used to be his grunge-o bedroom (nothing gross like pink but a sort of dark green) and turned it into *their* room. They bought a new bed and put curtains at the windows instead of those stupid roll-up shades that somehow either shot clear to the top of the window or never managed to move at all.

And right away, in some not-very-important ways, things did begin to change. I mean, take the business of drinking out of the orange juice carton, or wearing my favorite Orioles shirt three days in a row without washing it. But when I asked the guys at school, they all just groaned and said, "Mothers. They're like that."

And the best thing was, instead of me having to spend yet another vacation at MacCauley while Mitch finished up teaching summer school and then did whatever it is teachers do to get ready for regular school, I got to hang out with Casey. We'd either be at home or the Bread Basket or the pool, or sometimes at the garden center on account of Casey had this idea that yards were supposed to be filled with more than just grass.

Another plus was that Half-a-Loaf turned out to be a great cat and took to sleeping at the foot of my bed, almost from the beginning. So, okay, life did sort of change, and I'll admit that since the wedding Mitch and I didn't get to have as much time for just the two of us. But life was still totally okay.

Even with all that lovey-dovey stuff between Mitch and Casey. The hand-holding and kissy-face. That's because I mostly managed to tune it out.

But then one perfectly normal Thursday morning Casey looked up from the newspaper and said, "Hey, Ben, the social worker's coming today. Would you do something to your room before then? Nothing drastic—just so it's vermin free, okay?"

"What social worker? And why's he coming here?" I said.

"She. And it's because of the Chinese baby girl we're adopting."

"We are? When did you decide to do that?" But as I spoke things sort of jiggled in my head—*China. Baby. Adoption.*

"B-e-n," said Casey, stretching out my name. "Come on—how can you not know? We've been talking about this, right in front of you, ever since Mitch and I decided to get married."

And that quick I knew that this part of "down the road" was already here and that maybe there were things I should have been paying attention to. Like the times Mitch and Casey sat at the kitchen table, talking, talking, talking, and filling out a ton of boring-looking papers and forms that were spread out in front of them.

"How come?" I said after a while.

"Because we didn't want any secrets. We're a family and—"

"No—I mean, how come about the Chinese baby?" I said.

"Okay," said Casey, getting up to pour herself another cup of coffee. "Let's go back to the beginning—but I still can't believe this is all news to you. So, okay, before I met Mitch, and you, I wasn't at all sure I'd ever really find anyone special enough to spend my life with, but I knew that was no reason not to have a child. That's when I did a lot of research—I mean *a lot* of research—and decided to adopt a baby from China.

"I had already applied by the time I met you and Mitch. To tell you the truth, I thought about canceling, but I couldn't stop thinking about some child far away who was meant to be my daughter. So your father and I talked it over, and over, and over, and decided to redo the papers and to include Mitch's name on the application. But then what happened was that all the inspections that had been done at my apartment had to be redone because I live here now. The agency's being really great in trying to hurry things along. Which is why the social worker's coming today. Okay?"

I figured that "Okay?" was another one of those grownup questions that didn't need an answer, so I just nodded and made a promise to myself. From that moment on I would try to pay strict attention to everything anyone said in this family.

Casey must've called Mitch at MacCauley and told him about our conversation because when he got home he went through the whole thing all over again. He even pointed to a stack of books on the kitchen counter and asked how come I hadn't noticed that they were all about China. Big deal—like who checks out what his father is reading?

"So, Ben," Mitch finished up. "Do you have any questions?"

"Yeah," I said. "Will she—this kid—speak Chinese?"

"Well, we've asked for a very young child. She probably won't be talking yet, so she'll grow up speaking English. But we'll always want her Chinese culture to be a part of her life." Sometimes when my father talks, he really does sound like a schoolteacher—and this was one of those times. Anyway, then he went on to say, "What else can I tell you? You're bound to have a lot more questions."

I shook my head. "Not right now." I mean, my head was numb—but I guess shock will do that to you.

Not long after I started fifth grade, Casey and Mitch got what they called their referral. What that meant was that somewhere in China there really was a kid with their name on it. They even got pictures by e-mail, too. There was this little girl with fat cheeks and sticking-up hair and big wide-open eyes whose name was Mingmei, and she was headed this way. Except that Mitch and Casey had to go get her.

After that, the whole Chinese thing got really intense, what with tons more books, and maps, and Web sites. We even got to eat out a lot—at Chinese restaurants, of course.

Never
Say
Never

"Are you going to get to go to China?" Will asked one day when a bunch of us were on our way to French class. Will happens to be this guy I've known maybe forever and who's sort of Sam to me being Frodo—except that he would say that *I* was Sam and *he* was Frodo.

"Nooooo way," I said. "No way."

"How come?" asked Pedro, who I've also known forever and whose mother teaches at MacCauley so we've logged a lot of overtime together. "Because my mom has these friends who adopted a kid from China and when she, the kid, was about seven they went back to China for another child and took the older one with them."

"Yeah, well," I said, "maybe that was because the first kid was Chinese and it was sort of like going home for her. Anyway, you've got to know that my dad would never let me miss all that school. Never in a million years."

I should have known better than to say that though, because, as Aunt Jo is always saying, "Never say never." And it was that very night, just as we were finishing dinner, that Casey passed me a cookie and said, "You know, Ben, Mitch and I've been talking it over and, even though Jo and Charlie would love to have you stay with them, we really want you to go to China with us."

"Me? China?" I squawked. "I've never even been to New York City and you want me to go to China?"

"Yes. After all, this *is* a family thing," said Mitch. "And we're a family."

"Yeah, but me in China? On an airplane? For how long? And what about school?" The questions kept spilling out of me.

"We'll be gone just over two weeks," said Casey.

"And I've already talked to Joe Lawrence about your being absent from school, and he agrees with me—that this is an opportunity not to be missed."

Now, Mr. Lawrence is the principal at MacCauley and the final word on everything—at least everything to do with school, and a lot more, if you ask me.

"It will be an amazing experience," said Casey, reaching for another cookie. "The flight over will be long, but once we're there it'll be . . ."

Casey talked on, but by then the idea of two weeks off from school had kicked in and I figured it'd be like getting fourteen snow days lumped together. I even managed to squash down any thoughts of homework that would have to be made up. But China? It might be okay except for that Chinese baby we'd be schlepping around with us.

"Hey," I said. "How about the three of us do the China thing first and *then* pick up the Mingmei kid, just in time to come home?"

Casey laughed and Mitch gave me one of those fake punches on the arm that's supposed to mean, "Good joke, Ben."

"It doesn't work that way," said Casey. "We'll get her almost as soon as we arrive, but afterward there'll be plenty of time to do all the things we want to do."

I must've still been shaking my head over the whole thing because my father plunked a stack of books about China on the table in front of me and said, "You look like you're in a daze, Ben. And I'm sure you've got a ton of questions, so just fire away."

I'll bet anything that what Mitch and Casey expected was a bunch of travel questions, like "How long will it take to get there?" and "What's the weather like?" and "Where exactly *is* China?" But what I asked about was something that had been bugging me since this whole thing began.

"What I don't understand," I said, eyeing the plate of cookies, then turning away so I could concentrate on what I was about to say, "what I don't understand at all is why, if you guys wanted to get a kid, you went for a *girl* baby instead of a boy baby? Or even an older boy? Like my age, or maybe a bit younger." I sat back to think about how a brother might actually be a *good* thing to have.

24

My thinking time was immediately cut short. I mean, it was like *pow*—if I'd given them bugles and a drumroll, I couldn't have provided a better introduction for the *history lesson*.

"You see, Ben, it's like this," said Casey. "Throughout Chinese history, girls have never been valued as they should have been."

Right off I was tempted to make some smart-aleck remark, but somehow the look on my father's face told me to keep my mouth shut.

"And at the end of the Chairman Mao era," Mitch went on, as if I had any idea who this Chairman Mao dude even was, "population control became very important for the People's Republic of China. By 1980, they had established the one-child policy."

"Which meant," Casey added, "that often mothers would resort to hiding their daughters, or giving them up, so they would still have a chance to have a son. And while occasionally a boy is put up for adoption, most of the children available from China are girls." Casey's face looked streaky and sad as she went on. "Because boys were better able to work in the fields, and also to take care of their parents when they got old."

"But that's not fair," I said, sitting bolt upright. "For Chairman Whoever-he-is to tell people what kids they could have."

"Exactly," said Mitch.

"And even though the policy has eased a bit, there are

still an awful lot of abandoned little girls in China. Just waiting," said Casey. "That's why we're going to China. And because your dad and I really want another child."

Which pretty much did it for the history lesson except that before I could get away from the table, Mitch whipped a fat green book out of the pile and handed it to me. "Read this, Ben. It'll explain it as well as anyone can." And I noticed the yellow Post-it notes were already attached, like maybe the teacher part of my father had just been ready for me.

From then on we were into practical stuff. The *getting* season, I called it. Getting things, getting ready, getting shots.

The getting-things part came first and was sort of easy, mostly because friends of Mitch and Casey gave them a baby shower and brought a ton of presents (all for the Chinese baby). I mean, there we were, drowning in pajamas and shirts and overalls and dresses and stuffed teddy bears.

Then the big things began to appear. All of a sudden, there was a crib in what used to be the spare room, a high chair in the kitchen, and a stroller in the garage.

Somewhere along the way, Mitch took me to apply for a passport, which made the going-to-China thing seem incredibly real. Then Casey took me shopping for new underwear and socks and jeans without holes in them, and even an Orioles sweatshirt.

The getting-ready part was pretty much up to Mitch

and Casey and had to do with stopping newspapers and mail and finding someone to take care of Half-a-Loaf.

And as for the getting-shots business, there's not much I can say except *ouch*.

Then there was the whole thing about a name for the kid. I mean, she already had one that she was bringing with her: Mingmei, which was kind of weird but okay, as far as I was concerned. But out of nowhere Mitch and Casey were totally involved in some giant find-the-perfect-name hunt.

Books began to appear in the house. Not China books, but ones with mile-long lists of names, and what they meant, and where they came from. Both Mitch and Casey spent hours on the Internet visiting name-the-kid Web sites, and every evening at dinner, instead of having conversations, we bounced around names like so many rubber balls.

Emily, Meaghan, Jessica, Brittany, Laura, Elizabeth, Jane, Julia, Maria.

"But her name is Mingmei—how come she needs another?" I asked one night when we'd run through the list of possibilities for about the seventy-fifth time.

"That's her Chinese name," said Casey. "And of course we'll keep that, too, but she needs an American name. Now, *Mingmei* means 'smart and beautiful,' so we need something to go with that."

27

If you asked me (which no one did), "smart and beautiful" would be hard to mess up, so just about any name from any one of those lists should do. Besides, all that hoopla was beginning to make me think about *Benjamin* and whether, back before I was born, Mitch and Sara Jane had sat in this exact same room doing the exact same thing. And in a weird, creepy way, thinking that made me feel sort of sad and I yanked my thoughts back to the present. Where Mitch and Casey were still at it: *Emily, Meaghan, Jessica, Brittany.*

Later, when Mitch came into my room to say goodnight, I finally asked him, "Did you do that—you and my mother? I mean, did the two of you just sit around forever trying to find the perfect name—for me?"

For a minute Dad got one of those way-back looks on his face. Then he shook his head and said, "Not really, Ben. You see, from the minute we knew you were on the way, your mother and I seemed to know that you would be named after your two grandfathers, even though they were both already dead. It was important to us."

I thought about that for a while, about Benjamin and David, the grandfathers I never knew. And how being named after them was every bit as cool as if my parents had read a zillion name-the-baby books before I was born. After that, I pretty much forgot about the whole name thing and concentrated on getting ready for China.

Then, on the Sunday before we left, when Aunt Jo and Uncle Charlie and Nanny and Fred were all there to say goodbye, Casey stepped up onto a kitchen chair and announced, in a *ta-dum* kind of voice, "We have a name. As of this moment, our daughter and Ben's sister will be Maude Mingmei Mitchell."

Which, in my opinion, was a lot of *M*s. And *Maude*? What a thing to do to a kid. But I was smart enough not to say any of this out loud, which was a good thing, on account of it turned out that Maude had been the name of Casey's grandmother, the same one who gave her those dishes a long time ago, who happened to be dead now but who Casey had always thought was a real cool lady.

Looking back, it seemed that a lot had gone on since that day on the way to French class when I told Will that no way was I going to China. And I still wasn't sure if this whole baby thing would end up fitting into the all-right or not-all-right column, according to my philosophy of life.

China

China was the greatest. Cool. And I don't mean weather-cool but, you know, all around.

There were mountains and temples, and everybody was using chopsticks—but the way they are supposed to be used and not the way I did when I tried it at home. There were people riding three wheel bikes and lots of markets and funky green vegetables. There were places called teahouses and dragon pictures everywhere and tons of rice and noodles. And one thing I discovered was that since there's no alphabet in China, when Chinese kids learn to read and write they have to memorize about a gazillion characters, which all looked like squiggly bits of writing to me. I'm sure I could never remember what any of them meant.

But wait. I'm getting ahead of myself. I mean, first we had to get there. And before that, we had to pack, and this almost led to a total family meltdown. That's on account of the things we had to take for the kid, like diapers and formula, and a mountain of clothes, and even extra clothes to leave at the orphanage, as a sort of present.

And for every bit of baby stuff we put in the suitcases (and in my duffel bag), something important had to be left home. Like my very favorite mushed-down high-tops with the extra-long laces.

I can't remember much about the flight over because I slept most of the way. I mean, I'd wake up from time to time and look at the movie flickering on the pull-down screen, but then I'd go back to sleep. I'd bet anything though that Mitch and Casey sat wide-eyed all night, just waiting to get there and meet the Mingmei kid.

And then we arrived and it was like *wow*. As soon as we'd collected our bags and gone through customs and all that, we met up with our group—the other people who were adopting kids and who we'd be with the whole time we were in China. It (the group) was mostly made up of couples except for one single mom, which is what Casey would've been if she hadn't married Mitch and me. There was a six-year-old Chinese girl, too, coming back to help her mother and father get another kid. And there was me.

And on the way to the hotel we saw both a McDonald's and a KFC, which was reassuring in a way.

Once we got there, our room at the hotel was definitely okay, until I found out it was for all of us—me, Mitch, Casey, and even the baby when we got her. As for the rest of that day, Mitch and Casey slept and I sat by the window, looking down at the traffic and waiting for something to happen.

Which it definitely did the next day. Once breakfast

was done, we were herded into a big room downstairs in the hotel. After that, it wasn't long before a bunch of caretaker types arrived, with armloads of babies stuffed into snowsuit kinds of things. Then, one by one, the families were asked to come forward, and when it got to be Mitch and Casey's turn they both grabbed hold of me and the three of us went up.

From then on, it gets kind of blurry. I remember someone handing a baby to Casey. I remember Mitch putting one hand on the kid's head and the other on my shoulder. And I remember Casey leaning over and saying, "Maudie Mingmei, here's your brother, Ben. And Ben, here's your new sister."

Who, me? I still wasn't sure about this whole brother/ sister thing, but right then something so totally awesome happened to Casey's face that it made me blink and swallow hard. Something that never happened to it at the Bread Basket or when she was home with Mitch and me. Or even in the ninth inning of the most super-important Orioles game you could imagine. Then I looked over at Mitch and the same thing had happened to him. I mean, there were the two of them looking all shiny and soft and sort of goofy.

After the children had been handed out, we took Maudie Mingmei back to our room and Casey started peeling layers and layers of clothes off of her. You'd have thought we'd gotten an Eskimo baby. Then Casey put her in some of the things we'd brought, a white ruffly shirt and pink overalls with Oshkosh on them. And there she was with her fat cheeks and wide-awake eyes and that sticking-up hair, same as in the picture, and when I leaned over close to her she caught hold of my nose and wouldn't let go.

We did a lot while we were in China. Some of it was business and had to do with the adoption, like getting a visa application and taking Maudie Mingmei to the medical clinic for a checkup. But we did fun things, too. We went to parks and department stores, and even to tiny shops with signs that said "Welcome, Adoption Parents." We met strangers on the street who smiled a lot and pinched Maudie Mingmei's cheeks. A few of them even pinched mine.

And I learned to say one thing in Chinese: *Nie hao, nie hao*. It's a greeting, sort of like hi, though in the beginning I always thought people were saying hee-haw, hee-haw.

Then before we knew it, it was time for the big night-before-we-go-home dinner, with a ton of food, including ostrich meat. The next day at the airport, though we were all heading back to the United States on the same plane, there was a lot of crying and hugging and carrying on, and that's when Casey said something about all that Mingmei was leaving behind.

And right then it hit me, and I thought well, yeah, she really *is* leaving a ton of stuff behind, like this whole big country and the dragon pictures and the squiggly way of writing. And for the first time ever I thought about the woman who had been her birth mother and who had had to give her up and how she would probably always think about that sticking-up-hair baby.

It was weird, but I thought about how even though it was sad, it was happy, too. Because now Casey and Mitch and I had this kid. Maudie.

The
Not-All-Right

The trip home seemed to last longer than the whole time we were in China. As soon as we got onto the plane I just slumped down in my seat, planning to sleep my way back to Baltimore. But what I hadn't figured on were the babies—eleven of them.

And babies cry.

They didn't all cry at once though. I mean, that might have made some kind of sense. Sort of like if there'd been an orchestra onboard and the conductor swooped his baton at the whole crowd of babies at the same time and signaled for them to cry. After enough of that, he'd have gone on to the flutes and cellos and violins. And the babies would've kept quiet.

Hah.

These kids took turns, like maybe they'd worked it out among themselves before we left China. I mean, if Maudie cried and Casey and Mitch jiggled her and bounced her and cooed at her and she finally dozed off, then, at that very moment, a kid three rows back and on the other side of the plane would start up. And by the time her parents got her to stop, it was the turn of some-one two rows forward and in the middle. And that's the way it went—round and round the plane, till it was time for Maudie to cry again.

We had a two-hour layover in Chicago, where I ate three pieces of pepperoni pizza and stocked up on peanut M&M's and where there were more goodbyes, and more hugging and crying on account of we were the only fam-ily going to Baltimore. And by the time we got on that plane, Maudie (the only baby this time) just scrunched up and slept the whole way. But by then the damage was done. When we went up the ramp and stepped into the terminal at BWI, Mitch and Casey and I looked like something out of a horror movie. Maudie, on the other hand, was wide-awake with a giant smile on her face.

At first it felt as though we were rock stars, what with such a great mob of people waiting for us that late Sun-day afternoon. I saw Aunt Jo and Uncle Charlie and even Stan and Scott, both at college now but home for the weekend, and Nanny and Fred, too. Then about skatey-gazillion more people came surging forward—all Casey's relatives. And I have to say, they way outdid the China group in the hugging and kissing department. In fact, if you ask me, there was a lot more hugging and kissing than I thought was absolutely necessary. I mean, they didn't just go for Casey and Mitch and Maudie Mingmei, but for me, too. Which was definitely gross.

Another thing: it suddenly seemed as if I had a whole

new identity. I wasn't just Ben anymore. Or even Benjamin David or Benjamin David Mitchell. I was *the big brother*.

The trouble was that I was so tired and felt like such a zombie I seemed to be looking at everyone through a thick wall of fog and, except for Aunt Lois from the wedding, I never managed to hook names onto any of them. And all those people who'd come from places like Delaware and Pennsylvania to welcome us back didn't seem any realer to me than the strangers going up and down on the escalators.

Anyway, we stood there in the airport for a while with everybody talking at once and with Aunt Jo and Nanny and Casey's fog-relatives passing Maudie around, like maybe she was a football. As if that wasn't bad enough, every time I tried to slither off, to find a chair or a wall to lean on, someone would pull me back. "How did you like China?" they wanted to know. "Don't you just love your baby sister?" And, over and over, "How's it feel to be *the big brother*?"

Eventually we managed to get our luggage and make our way outside and say goodbye to Stan and Scott, who were heading to town in Scott's car, and to Casey's gazillion relatives—whose names I still didn't know. Then we piled into Fred's and Uncle Charlie's cars, but when we got to our house I could really tell that Aunt Jo and Nanny wanted to settle down for some kind of extended visit. Maybe it's because of the way one and then the other of them kept saying, "Oh, we can't wait to spend time with this beautiful baby and to hear everything about your trip."

"These people are exhausted," said Fred. "We should clear out of here and let them rest."

"Well, yes, you're right," said Nanny. "But maybe just a short visit."

"Plenty of time for visiting tomorrow, when you bring Half-a-Loaf back," said Uncle Charlie, taking Aunt Jo by the arm and leading her toward the door. "Tomorrow and the day after and the day after that."

Then they were gone and it was just the four of us—Casey, Mitch, the kid, and me. Right away Casey started showing Maudie around and saying stuff like "Here's Maudie's living room, and Maudie's dining room, and here's the sunporch with the TV, and in here's the kitchen."

And that's when I found out the best-ever thing about relatives: they bring food. Before going to the airport, a bunch of them must have stopped by the house and filled the refrigerator. There was a whole cooked chicken and potato salad and applesauce and milk and orange juice and, in the freezer, ice cream. There was a plate of cookies on the counter and a chocolate cake, too. And best of all, no rice or noodles anywhere in sight. No ostrich either.

After we ate, we went to bed and for once we weren't

all jumbled into the same hotel room. I figured if Maudie Mingmei cried in the night, that would be her parents' problem because one thing I knew for sure—I didn't plan to hear her. That was definitely not in the job description of *the big brother*.

The
Good and
the Bad

Okay, I know Mitch said there were going to be some changes in our lives—but *this* many? Partly they were because of my dad marrying Casey, but mostly they had to do with getting Maudie.

"I should've warned you," said Will one day when he and Pedro and I had settled into our sunporch with the entire Risk: Lord of the Rings game spread out on the floor in front of us. "First off, you got to watch 'em every minute—even when you're not watching 'em." With that he nodded toward Maudie, who was halfway across the room turning pages of a cloth book and chewing on some green floppy thing called a Wiggle Worm. "You'll find this out for yourself, but little kids can get from there to here quicker'n you can blink an eye."

"Yeah," said Pedro. "And you got to be ready to hurl your body on top of your belongings and hang on for dear life."

With that Maudie dropped the Wiggle Worm and shot across the floor, half crawling and half slithering, reaching out for the pile of cards. And that quick, Will and Pedro were flat on the floor, covering the board with their bodies, protecting orcs, elven archers, dice, and even the ring.

"That's enough, Miss Maudie Mitchell," said Casey, appearing in the doorway and coming over to swoop Maudie up. "Let's give the boys some peace and quiet, though they might want to move that onto the kitchen table. But, Will and Pedro, you guys should be used to this, right?"

"Yeah," said Will, adding, once Casey and Maudie were out of the room, "that's one reason I always liked coming here."

"*Used* to like it," said Pedro. "It was so *quiet*. So sort of *civilized* here."

Whenever we had a choice, we liked to hang out at my place because of Will's two younger sisters and Pedro's three-year-old twin brothers. This had automatically turned the two of them into genuine Kid Experts.

"Anyway," I said, as we scooped up handfuls of dark riders and cave trolls so we could move the game into the kitchen, "I thought babies stayed in cribs most of the time. And slept a lot, or sat in one of those bouncy chairs making funny noises."

"Hah!" said Pedro.

"Well, they do, sort of. In the beginning," Will said. "But how old was Maudie when you guys got her?"

"Almost a year," I said. "Eleven months and something. I remember because we had her birthday almost as soon as we got back from China."

"See," said Pedro, jabbing his finger at me. "She did a lot of crib time over there, and now that she's here, she's ready to go. But it'll get worse—wait till she actually starts *walking*. Babies are okay, but they change stuff, too. You'll find out."

And I was catching on fast. About those big clunky car seats that were stuck like warts in the backseats of both Casey's and Mitch's cars. About finding rubber ducks and plastic blocks in the bottom of the tub every time I went to take a shower, and Cheerios and glops of applesauce on the kitchen floor that made walking in my bare feet feel totally gross. And about hearing the words "Not so loud—the baby's sleeping" whenever I so much as breathed.

But even with all that, life eventually returned to the way it had been before the kid. Mitch went back to Mac-Cauley. Casey went back to the Bread Basket, taking Maudie along until she did actually learn to walk, then dropping her at day care.

Spring came and soccer started and now it wasn't just Mitch at my games, or Mitch and Casey, but Maudie Mingmei, too. And Nanny and Fred had started to come sometimes, which made it way cool—having a real family there, I mean, and hearing them yell "Go, Ben" as I raced up and down the field. But then, afterward, instead of

Mitch and me heading to the diner for our regular burger or bowl of chili, we all just came home. Because Maudie had to go to bed.

Then there was the Science Competition and my great humiliation. The Science Competition is this thing—sort of like a spelling bee, only with science questions—that happens at MacCauley every year. The miracle was that I ever got picked to be in it, science not exactly being what Aunt Jo would call my strong suit. Anyway, it was late on a Sunday afternoon and I had somehow made it to the fourth round and the questions were getting harder and, if you ask me, trickier.

"Now, Ben," said Mr. Lawrence, his principal-voice booming through the auditorium, "your next question is, 'A huge sea wave caused by a great disturbance under an ocean such as an earthquake or volcanic eruption is called . . .' "

I stood up tall, the way Mrs. Savopoulos had told us to. I took a humongous deep breath and dug back into my brain, reaching, reaching for the answer. I could feel it there, could almost touch it, and I dug deeper, pretty sure it started with a *t*, or maybe an *s*. Just as the answer drifted into my consciousness, just as I was about to pluck it up and say it out loud, I heard a voice from somewhere out in the crowd.

"Wog, wog, wog, wog," Maudie sang out her version of *frog*. Her words sailed around the room and bounced off the walls, but more than that, they echoed through my head. *Wog, wog, wog* over and over until, almost without knowing I was doing it, I called out my answer.

"A frog," I said. And everybody laughed.

"Sorry, Ben," said Mr. Lawrence, swallowing a laugh of his own. "That is incorrect."

And I went back to my seat and stared at a crack in the floor and felt my face burn as if it was on fire.

When the Science Competition was over, Mitch, Casey, and Maudie were waiting for me in the hall. Mitch shook my hand and told me I did well, then made one of those dumb parent remarks about how it was an honor to be chosen. And I glared at him.

Casey gave me a hug and whispered, "I'm sorry, Ben." I glared at her, too.

And just when I was about to extend my glare to the kid, who was bouncing up and down in Casey's arms, Maudie lunged forward, shoving some stupid stuffed green frog in my face and saying, "Wog, wog, wog."

And, in spite of myself, I had to laugh.

One day after soccer practice, the coach handed out brochures for this really cool summer camp in West Virginia that Will and Pedro and a bunch of the other guys were definitely one hundred percent going to go to. But when I gave the flyer to Mitch, he hemmed and hawed and pulled on his ear the way he does when he's not sure about something, and right away I knew that soccer camp was disappearing into that great land of *We'll see*.

Suddenly spring was done and fifth grade was over and it was summer. By then Maudie wasn't just walking but running and jumping and climbing, too. Her vocabulary still seemed stuck on *fwoggy*, though. And *Mau-Mau* (Maudie). And *Ben*. Anyway, Mitch and I cut the grass and trimmed the bushes, and Casey planted tomatoes and Shasta daisies. On nice nights we ate out back and Mitch burned chicken and burgers and sometimes steak, and I pretty much knew that this was the way summer was going to be.

Except that every once in a while I'd ask Mitch about soccer camp. And each time I did, he'd pull on his ear and say, "I'm trying to work it out, Ben."

The thing was, much as I wanted to go, I didn't have to be a rocket scientist to know that that trip to China was all the vacation any of us were going to get for a long, long time. Till I heard about the week we were going to spend in Chicken. Or Turkey. Or wherever.

who's
who

Duck," said Casey. She and Mitch and I were sitting out back at the picnic table eating s'mores and listening to Maudie shout her latest word, *Moo*, from upstairs in her crib.

We'd finished supper and partway cleaned up, and now we were just hanging out, watching it get dark and waiting for the fireflies to appear. Mitch and Casey were talking and, despite my resolution about paying attention to family stuff, I'd been spacing out again. Until I heard the tag end of something that sounded like ". . . great spending all that time at the beach."

"What time? Which beach? Where?" I asked, coming back to earth with a thud.

And that's when Casey said, "Duck." Followed by, "It's in North Carolina, on the Outer Banks."

"What about it?" I said, smooshing the rest of my s'more into my mouth.

"Well, it's where a lot of people in my family go every year for their vacation, only *this* year, because it's Fred and Nanny's fiftieth wedding anniversary, they've rented three houses and are taking *all* of us for a week."

"Who?" I said, looking from Casey to Mitch and back to Casey again.

"Us. You and Mitch and Maudie and me. My brothers and sisters and brothers-in-law and sisters-in-law and their kids. Everybody," she said. "The family."

"The ones who were at the airport, you mean?"

"More," said Casey. "All of us. The whole entire family."

And right away it was like some kind of instant explosion in my head. That's because the idea of going from just Aunt Jo and Uncle Charlie and two much older cousins to practically the world as family will do that to you.

"And it's like a *real* beach?" I asked. "With sand and waves and rides and everything?"

"A real beach," said Mitch. "No rides, but it's really a great place—you'll love it."

"Yeah, well, maybe . . . I guess," I said, stumbling over my words while I tried to get my head around the idea of three houses filled with a gazillion people who, even if I'd met some of them before, I didn't really *know*. Making them practically *strangers*. "So when *is* this?"

"The first week in August," said Casey, reaching out and cupping a firefly in her hands, then letting it go.

That's when I froze, right there on the bench of the

picnic table, on account of the first week in August was *the exact same time as soccer camp.*

"The first week of August?" I croaked. "You're sure it's the *first* week?" And the whole time I was gagging over these words, a bunch of pictures seemed to be flashing around me—pictures of Will and Pedro and probably everybody else I know off in West Virginia having a blast and living in tents and building bonfires and playing nonstop soccer. "I'm going to Chicken for the first week of August?"

"Duck," said Mitch. "And yes, you are. We all are." Then he gave me a nudge with his foot under the table (actually, it was more of a kick) and went on. "As Casey told you, it's Nanny and Fred's anniversary. And fifty years is a really big deal."

And right off, that made me think of my mother, Sara Jane, and how she'd only been married three years before she died. I was sitting there trying to figure out why that made me feel sort of sad, on account of it's hard to be sad about someone you can't remember, when the *moo*s coming from Maudie's crib turned into fussing and then to crying.

"I'll go see what's wrong," said Casey, getting up and heading for the door.

"I'm sorry, Ben," my father said, once he was sure Casey was all the way in the house. "I know you really wanted to go to soccer camp—and I'd hoped we could've worked it out."

"We still could," I said, kicking at the table leg. "I mean, I'll just go to soccer camp and you guys can go to boring old wherever. And with those tons of people, you won't even know I'm not there."

"I would know, and I'd miss you," said Mitch. "But it's more than that. The point is that this is really going to be a great family week—and we're a family. Casey and you and Maudie and I. And Casey and I both think it's important for us to be together."

"They're not my family—no way. And besides, what about what's important to *me*?"

"They *are* your family because they're Casey's—and *we're* Casey's family. Anyway, Ben, I think we have to consider the greater good here—what's good for us as a whole." And with that Mitch got up and headed over to clean the grill, and I sat there staring down at a blob of marshmallow and giving the table leg one final kick, just for good measure. I thought about how this whole family thing had a lot of togetherness hooked onto it. I mean, I liked Casey, but I would have liked her better if she hadn't come equipped with so many relatives. I liked Maudie Mingmei, too, but sometimes I couldn't help wishing that it was just Mitch and me again. For a little while anyway.

And now I had this monster vacation staring me in the face. With the monster family that I was pretty sure was made up of a bunch of orcs—and trolls—and wargs. In Duck.

• • •

In the next few weeks it seemed like the only thing we heard about was Duck. As in who was staying in which house with what relatives. And did everybody want to buy food here and lug it down, or should they go to the Food Lion once they got there. And how about sheets and towels, and was there an outdoor shower at each house.

Meanwhile, since I figure it's always good to identify the enemy, I made it my project to figure out who these people were—the ones I'd be spending my so-called vacation with. So I started asking questions, grilling Casey, putting her through the third degree, with "How many sisters do you have?" and "How many brothers?" and "Do they all have kids?" and "Do you know each and every name?" and "Who's the oldest—kid, I mean?" and "Is Maudie the youngest?"

Then Casey would toss out things like "You met my sister Lois at the wedding" and "Tom does magic tricks" and "My brother George's twins are sixteen now."

Eventually, when I thought I had it sorted out, I put the whole great mob of relatives together on a chart. The trouble was, even while I was doing it, I knew that not one of them was going to come close to being as much fun as soccer camp.

Anyway, here's what I found out:

CASEY'S FAMILY

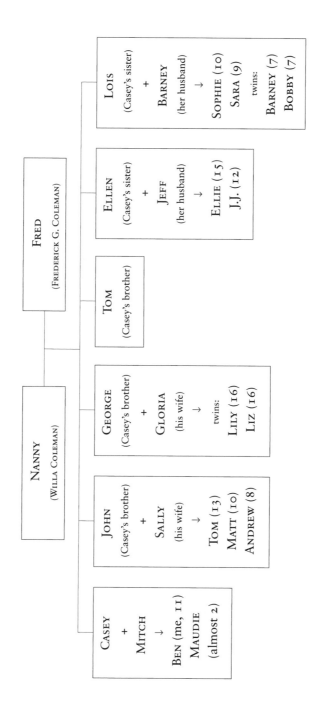

NANNY
(WILLA COLEMAN)

FRED
(FREDERICK G. COLEMAN)

CASEY
+
MITCH
→
BEN (me, 11)
MAUDIE
(almost 2)

JOHN
(Casey's brother)
+
SALLY
(his wife)
→
TOM (13)
MATT (10)
ANDREW (8)

GEORGE
(Casey's brother)
+
GLORIA
(his wife)
→
twins:
LILY (16)
LIZ (16)

TOM
(Casey's brother)

ELLEN
(Casey's sister)
+
JEFF
(her husband)
→
ELLIE (15)
J.J. (12)

LOIS
(Casey's sister)
+
BARNEY
(her husband)
→
SOPHIE (10)
SARA (9)
twins:
BARNEY (7)
BOBBY (7)

Poornora

"Is this everybody?" I asked, handing my chart to Casey as we were sitting on the porch of the Bread Basket one afternoon. We'd been taking an end-of-the-day break and sampling a new kind of raisin bread, to see if it was as good as the regular one.

"Wow, it *is* a lot of people, when you see it written out like that," she said, counting names. "That's it. Twenty-six." She started to hand it back, then caught herself. "Wait a minute, you forgot—or I guess I forgot to tell you—Poornora."

"Poor-who?" I said, choking on the second piece of bread I'd just popped into my mouth.

"Poornora," said Casey.

"What's a Poornora?"

"Not what—who." She shook her head and her face looked like a day where it had been sunny but wasn't any-more. "She's my aunt, from New Jersey."

"Oh," I said. "And her name is *Poornora*?"

"Not really. In fact, I guess her name is just

plain Nora, except that she's always been Poornora."

"How come?" I asked, taking a slug of lemonade and trying to decide if I needed another piece of raisin bread. To make sure it was as good as I thought it was. "How come you call her that?"

"Everybody does," said Casey. "It's hard to explain, but she's sort of the kind of person things happen to."

"Bad things?" I said.

"Not really extra bad, but whatever happens always *seems* especially bad because of the way she reacts. Just kind of gloomy. And because of that, people were always saying things like 'Poor Nora this' and 'Poor Nora that.' Then when my older brothers, George and John, were young, they kept hearing about Poor Nora and decided that was her name—one word. So when the rest of us came along we just called her that, and after a bit the grownups took it up, and that's who she became: Poornora."

"Does she care?" I asked. "About being called Poornora?"

"That's what's so totally weird," said Casey. "My aunt really is a bundle of contradictions, and for some reason she thinks Poornora is an okay name. She even signs birthday cards to all of us that way."

"That's kind of bizarre, but still, what's it have to do with my chart?" I asked.

Casey sighed. "It has to do with your chart because

my mother has invited *her* to go to Duck with the rest of *us*."

"Nanny has?" I said.

"Nanny has," said Casey, sighing again. "Poornora'll come down from New Jersey by train, spend a couple of days with my parents beforehand, and then go on to Duck with them. And she'll be staying at house number one with Nanny and Fred and you and Mitch and Maudie and me."

Before I could think of what to say, a car pulled up and a woman got out, coming onto the porch and asking about olive bread. I trailed Casey and the woman into the store, and after that a man came wanting brownies and another woman looking for a Bundt cake. It went on like that, really busy till closing time, so I didn't get a chance to quiz Casey about Poornora again till we had locked up the Bread Basket and were on our way to get Maudie at day care.

"So tell me more about this Poornora person," I said once we were in the car.

"Well," said Casey, "as I told you, she's Nanny's sister. Her twin sister."

"Her twin? That's cool." As I said that, part of my brain was thinking how two of Nanny couldn't be all bad. The other part was thinking that with so many twins in Casey's family it's a wonder she hadn't come home from China with an extra kid. "Does she look like Nanny?" I asked.

"Not really. Or maybe a little bit. You know those masks you sometimes see on theaters with one face laughing and one face frowning—well, they could be my mother and Poornora."

"But what *about* her?" I said. "Does she have kids and grandkids and a husband? What does she *do*? And how come Nanny and Fred are bringing her?"

"Let's see," said Casey, stopping for a red light. "What about Poornora. Well, she says things like 'There's lots of news, but it's all bad.' She carries an umbrella when it isn't even supposed to rain and keeps her shades drawn so the sun won't fade her rugs.

"She was married to Uncle Oscar, who was a really nice man and who died last year. Her only daughter, my cousin Maureen, lives in Oregon and doesn't come home very often.

"She likes birds and bugs and nature things. And I think the reason my parents invited her to come to Duck is that they think they've been blessed that they've had so much. And they feel sorry for her. You know, like poor Poornora.

"But believe me, Ben. My mother and Poornora are nothing alike."

Which was decidedly not good news. I mean, ever since I've known her, I've thought Nanny was pretty cool. The opposite of that would make Poornora definitely *un*cool. Maybe even a super orc.

And I was sharing a house with her.

•   •   •

News flash: This so-called vacation that was happening during the exact same week as soccer camp just got a whole lot worse.

Duck

If you ask me, getting to Duck took longer than getting to China. Or at least it seemed that way.

But even before that, just as with China, we had to do the whole packing deal, which in this case meant piling everything we could ever possibly need into the dining room, ready to go. Mountains and mountains of beach chairs, beach towels, Boogie Boards and about 632 plastic sand buckets and shovels and sifter things for Maudie. Bags of groceries, bags of books, my *Lord of the Rings* DVDs and you-know-who's *Sesame Street* ones. Maudie's port-a-crib, booster seat, and a folding gate to keep her in or out, up or down. And that whole collection didn't even include our suitcases and duffel bags filled with bathing suits and flip-flops and sweatshirts (plus underwear and socks).

Then, once everything was assembled, Mitch and I had the fun of trying to load it all into the *great shrinking station wagon*. Which, up to now, had always been plenty big enough.

While Casey and Maudie took Half-a-Loaf over for

his vacation with Aunt Jo, my dad and I packed the car. It had to be done the night before so we could get *an early start*. Which turned out to mean dawn, when the sky was still a pinky kind of gray and the birds weren't even awake. And I'll bet anything that when we pulled out of the neighborhood our car looked like an overstuffed submarine sandwich on wheels, with bits of ham and cheese and pickles sticking out from everywhere. Except, of course, there was no one to see us because they were still asleep.

Then we drove. And drove. And drove. Only sometimes we stopped, then drove some more. Not always in the right direction because I *know for a fact* that we crossed the Elizabeth River three times at the same place. Back and forth and back again. Or is it forth and back and forth again.

Mitch and Casey had those tight-lipped looks on their faces that grownups get when they're trying to pretend that something is fun when it really isn't. Maudie took turns fussing and sleeping and shouting "Duck" and what we thought was "Fortune cookie" but probably wasn't. And as for me—I thought about West Virginia and soccer camp and how I wasn't there.

Eventually we turned off the highway, crossed a bridge, and, in a bit, headed north on Route 12, where all at once the air smelled sandy and salty and beachy. After that, Casey started reading signs, first calling out the numbered streets and then the ones with names like Periwinkle and Tuckahoe till she got to Sea Hawk and let out a yelp just as Mitch swung the car to the right and up the street. The closer we got to the ocean, the more the street seemed to be swarming with people, shouting and waving and running along beside us. And the thing was—you probably already guessed it—they were all related to Casey.

Just then, an incredible going-down-for-the-third-time feeling swept over me. That's because the minute I climbed out of the car and tried to straighten up (not easy to do when you've ridden skatey-eight hours with a Boogie Board hanging over your head and a duffel bag under your feet), I was drowning in relatives. And right away they started in with the hugging and kissing. Double-yuck—somebody even patted me on the head.

Plus, every one of them was talking at once.

". . . the trip down . . ."

". . . stopped for lunch . . ."

"The waves are awesome . . ."

". . . forgot her bathing suit . . ."

"Plenty of sunblock and . . ."

A kid stepped forward from out of the crowd, holding a video camera and swooping it up and down and from side to side, taking in Casey and Maudie, my father trying to drag a cooler out of the back of the car, and me, still bent and crooked like a pretzel. "And here we have," the camera guy announced, "the Mitchells from Baltimore—Casey, Mitch, Ben, and Maudie. Would any one of you like to give us your first impression of Duck?"

With that, someone with a super-loud voice ("You remember my sister Lois," Casey whispered, poking me in the ribs) waved her hand in front of the camera and said, "Not now, J.J. Just let them get unpacked and find their way around." Then she told us that Nanny and Fred were walking on the beach and that we should just go on in and get settled. "Casey, you and Mitch are in the blue room with sunflowers, Maudie's in the one next to it, and Ben is on the lower level, in back of the room where the kids hang out."

Then, as quickly as they appeared, the relatives disappeared and Mitch and I and sometimes Casey set about unloading the car while Maudie ran around shouting "Duck."

Okay. It wasn't West Virginia, and I didn't want to be here, and I *definitely* didn't want to be with the super-smothering, octopus-armed, head-patting family—but the house itself was impressive. I mean, it had three levels, and porches where you could sit and look at the ocean, a big-screen TV and a DVD player and a volleyball court and a *really* small swimming pool out back. But, hey, I'd never lived in a house with a swimming pool before, so it met my definition of impressive.

Mitch and Casey unpacked while I chased Maudie around the top floor (which is where the living and dining areas and the kitchen were) and fed her an occasional Goldfish cracker from a bag I found open on the table.

Casey and my father finally came upstairs and I was just about to head for my own private quarters on the lower level (maybe never to come out again, at least until it was time to leave) when Nanny and Fred's dalmatian, Pongo, came galumping up the stairs. They were right behind him (only slower), and a bit after that, complete with huffing and puffing, a counterfeit Nanny appeared and I knew right off that she had to be Poornora.

This is the way it was. Both Nanny and the fake Nanny had on shorts, except that (even though she had some of those scritchy blue vein things on her legs) Nanny's shorts looked okay. Poornora's didn't (and they drooped). Nanny had on flip-flops and a T-shirt that said *Mexico* across the front; Poornora had on striped socks and sandals and a polka-dot blouse that was made of something slimy. Nanny's gray hair was sticking up every which way on account of the wind. Poornora was wearing a crinkly plastic rain bonnet, though it wasn't raining, or even cloudy.

Nanny smiled. Poornora didn't.

"You're here, you're here," said Fred, slapping Mitch on the back and kissing Casey and Maudie. I ducked—in case he was of the head-patting school of thought.

"How was your trip? Did you find your room all right? Now, how about something to eat, just to tide you over a bit." Nanny's words seemed to spill into the room.

With that, she scooped up Maudie Mingmei, holding her out to Poornora and saying, "And here's Mitch and Casey's baby."

"Hmmmph," said Poornora.

"Duck," said Maudie.

"And this is Ben," said Nanny, giving me a nudge forward. I stuck my hand out, then right away yanked it back; otherwise, it would've dangled there forever. Besides, I didn't even get a Poornora "Hmmmph."

"Well, Mitch," said Fred, heading to the sink for a glass of water, "did you all run into much traffic on the way down?"

"Nothing to speak of," my father said. "We got a really early start—right, Ben?"

"How was your trip, Mom?" asked Casey.

"Oh, fine. No problem," said Nanny, leading Maudie over to a giant wooden flamingo standing by the fireplace.

"We must not have been in the same car, then," sniffed Poornora. "I seem to remember a big tie-up just outside of Washington. And how about that roadwork? And I don't care what Fred says—the air conditioner in that car wasn't working properly. If I were you, I'd have it seen to."

"Well, we're here now," said Nanny. "And we're on *vacation*."

"The cleaning crew was still here when we arrived, cleaning up from last week's tenants," Poornora rattled on. "And I'm not a bit sure about that bed in my room—

it will probably give me a backache." Then, like some beady-eyed bird, the fake Nanny looked straight at me and said, "Well, boy, I guess you don't want to hear an old woman complain, do you?"

"I'd rather hear about the birds and bugs and plants and stuff that Casey says you're sort of into." The words came out of nowhere—in my voice.

And that's when Poornora got this really strange look on her face, same as Kevin Ramsey used to get in second grade when he wasn't sure whether kids were being nice or not nice. "You mean it?" she asked after a bit.

The thing was, I didn't exactly mean it, except that I figured it was better than listening to any more of her complaints. So, in a way, I guess I did mean it. "Yeah— yes, I do," I said.

Poornora leaned close and peered at me for what seemed like ages before she said, "All right, boy. First thing tomorrow morning. Let me know what room you're sleeping in—I'll rout you out of bed if you're not up."

Casey's
Family

I woke early the next morning, partly because I didn't like the idea of being "routed" out of bed by Poornora, and partly because there was so much from the night before that I still needed to think about. I'd meant to sort through it before I fell asleep, but what with the whole business of getting to Duck and unloading the car and seeing Casey's gazillion relatives all in one place, once I hit the bed I totally flaked.

So even though I was awake and meant to be up and moving B.P. (before Poornora), I lay there instead, staring at the ceiling but seeing a rerun of my first night in Duck that spun in an endless loop through my head, like maybe it was still going on.

First off, it was crowded. And noisy. Which, I came to find out, were both synonyms for *family* I just never knew about. And because it was *the first night of vacation*, all twenty-seven of us (twenty-six of them, plus me) crowded into Nanny and Fred's house for supper. And twenty-seven is a *lot* of people—way more than I would've ever thought when I was meeting bits and pieces of them along the way. Twenty-seven is a crowd, a mob, a horde. A monster family.

Another thing I learned was that everyone in Casey's family talked at once. And most everyone in Casey's family ran up and down the stairs, and some of them slammed doors, and a few seemed to clunk into things when they came into rooms. Fred liked to watch CNN more or less nonstop, but he had to turn it up really loud to drown out the people all talking at once. Uncle George and Aunt Gloria's twins, Liz and Lily, then turned their boom box up even louder—to drown out CNN.

Uncle John flew an orange-and-purple kite from off the second-floor porch while his kids, Tom (named after Uncle Tom—to make it even more confusing), Matt, and Andrew, dashed outside every time it swooped down and snagged on a bush—then tried to hand it back up to him. Casey shrieked (nonstop) *not to dare let Maudie out on that porch by herself.* Uncle Tom, Casey's bachelor brother, did magic tricks and was all the time finding quarters in people's ears. Poornora sat in the corner, facing away from all of us and turning pages of a magazine.

J.J. ran through with his video camera, zooming in for close-ups and asking everyone for what he called "cool comments." At one point I saw Nanny grab him and point in my direction, but instead of coming my way he ran downstairs to help Tom, Matt, and Andrew with the kite. Or maybe see what they had to say for the camera. Seven-year-old Bobby spilled root beer on the rug, and his twin brother, Barney, stepped in it. The dog ate half a bowl of popcorn, then made disgusting heaving noises before he threw up on the rug, next to the root beer. Sophie and Sara and Ellie tried to play Twister in the living room till someone chased them into Nanny and Fred's bedroom. Mitch polished off almost a whole tray of spinach balls while talking to a guy who turned out to be Uncle Barney.

And in the kitchen Nanny, Casey, Aunt Gloria, Aunt Sally, and Uncle Jeff stepped back and forth around each other as they tried to get dinner on the table. Aunt Ellen, who was J.J.'s mother, sprawled on one of the living room couches, calling out from time to time, "It's too crowded in there—I'll help clean up." Aunt Lois passed me a bowl of peanuts and then suggested I go outside with the boys—but when I did, they had disappeared.

Dinner was awesome, though. I mean, there was a ton of lasagna and bread and a boatload of salad. The only trouble was, I just assumed that once we got our food, Mitch and Casey and Maudie and I would hunker down in a corner someplace and eat together. But when I looked for them, my dad was wedged between a couple of uncles on the couch and Casey and several aunts were pulled up next to Maudie's booster seat.

So I stood there looking like some dorky transfer student in the school cafeteria and wondering what to do. I mean, there wasn't a lot of choice with a bunch of *girls* sitting on the living room floor, the Bobby and Barney twins at the breakfast bar, and grownups everywhere else. All talking.

I could feel my face getting hotter and probably redder, and just as I was about to disappear down to the lower level, it was Uncle Tom to the rescue. As soon as he saw me standing there, he jumped up, snatched another quarter from behind my left ear, grabbed my plate, and led me out onto the porch. "Hey, guys," he said, putting my food on the picnic table, "you forgot someone."

"Hi," said J.J., moving over to make room for me.

"It's better out here," said Tom.

"No grownups," said Matt.

"But we have to keep sending someone in for food," said Andrew.

Mostly they talked about soccer and baseball games I hadn't been to and teams I'd never heard of, but it was okay, and when Tom went in after a while for peaches and brownies, he brought some back for me, too.

"Okay," said J.J., rolling his paper plate into a tube and holding it up to his eye, like maybe it was a telescope. "We all set for tomorrow?" Then pointing his plate at me, he said, "Seven-thirty tomorrow morning, in front of house number two. We're going to check this place out. Be sure and leave a note on the kitchen table though, 'cause Fred has this thing about knowing where people are. Also, we can hang out at the beach, but no swimming without the grownups there. So how about it—you with us?"

"Well, yeah, if . . . but . . . maybe . . ." I sounded like

a total wuss. But what was I supposed to say—that I already had plans? With *Poornora*?

The knock on my door was a no-nonsense kind of knock, same as Poornora's voice when she called, "You're late, boy. I'll be waiting out front—but don't you tarry."

Tarry? I pulled the pillow over my head and wondered what would happen if I just pretended not to hear her. I mean, would she leave me alone and go on by herself to check out the birds and bugs and stuff, or—

The second knock sounded like a shot. "Now, boy," said Poornora.

I rolled out of bed, thumping my feet on the floor to let her know I was awake, and grabbed up yesterday's clothes and put them on. After a quick bathroom stop I headed upstairs, figuring I could scarf down some breakfast and still get outside before Poornora came around for knock number three. But as I started up the steps, the house was so sort of middle-of-the-night quiet that I stopped and stood there for a minute, not sure what to do. Besides, I didn't know what the food rules were. I mean, could *anybody* eat *anything*, or were we just supposed to eat the stuff we brought? If so, how was I going to be able to tell our Cheerios from Nanny's or even Poornora's?

I was still trying to sort this out when I looked up and there was Poornora herself, complete with her plastic rain bonnet and with binoculars slung around her neck. She was standing on the porch and beckoning at me through the glass door.

Once outside, we went along the narrow boardwalk path, up the steps over the dune, and down onto the beach. The ocean stretched out in front of us, and the sun seemed to be sitting right on top of it, while up close the waves went *schroosh schroosh* against the shore. I dug my feet into the sand, took a giant breath, and more than anything I wanted to take off running. Except just at that moment Poornora snagged me with a question.

"Do you know where you are, boy?"

"On the beach."

"Where *is* the beach?"

For a minute I wanted to try the old *on Earth, in the solar system, in the universe* thing, but I figured that wouldn't go over too well. Instead, nudging a shell along with my foot, I mumbled, "In Duck."

"And what is Duck *on*, boy?"

Right off, I felt that I was flunking some kind of test. "Well, uh, on the edge of North Carolina maybe?" I said. "And besides, my name is Ben."

Poornora let out a *schroosh*ing sigh that sounded as loud as a breaking wave. "Barrier island, Ben. Barrier island—which runs parallel to the mainland shore. Hence 'Outer Banks.' "

And it sort of went along like that as Poornora and I made our way up the beach, me in my bare feet and her in those lace-up shoes that scritched against the sand. I kept looking out to sea and pretending I was Robinson Crusoe or somebody, alone on a desert island, and trying not to think about how hungry I was. Poornora kept up a steady stream of conversation about dunes and beach grass and some plant called dusty miller and whelks and clams and crabs.

"Do you know, Ben, that the gulls go for the whelks and clams but they're not able to bite the shells, so they fly up twenty feet or so and drop them on something hard—then eat what's inside." She finished up with a sort of *ta-dum* sound, then waited to see what I would say.

But before I could think of anything, I looked up and saw J.J., Tom, Matt, and Andrew running in a zigzag line toward us. And there I was—in total panic mode, not sure whether to head out to sea or burrow into the sand like one of the fiddler crabs Poornora had been going on about a while back. I doubled over, digging into the wet sand—digging, digging, digging—until I heard them go past.

"Did you know that, Ben? About the gulls and the whelks and the clams?"

"No, but that's pretty cool," I said, straightening up.

"All of nature is 'cool,' as you young people insist on saying," said Poornora as we made our way back to the house. "And tomorrow we'll talk about the birds."

Tomorrow, I thought, and all my insides sort of groaned. And *whaamo*, I remembered something Ms. Seegers, my fifth-grade English teacher, used to say a lot. Something about "Tomorrow, and tomorrow, and tomorrow" creeping in some kind of pace "from day to day . . ." Just then I saw my whole life, or at least my week in Duck, stretching out in front of me. And when we got to the house I made my escape, slipping around back and heading for the door to the lower level while Poornora stopped to get the sand out of her shoes. But as I came around the corner I almost fell over the boys, who were sitting on the ground with a box of doughnuts.

"Hey, where were you?" said J.J., holding the box out to me. "We waited a while, but then we left. Take a chocolate one—they're the best."

I picked out a fat, shiny chocolate doughnut and was just about to sink my teeth into it when Poornora came around the side of the house. "Ben, I've been thinking, and it should be your turn next time."

"My turn?" I croaked. "My turn for what?"

"To teach *me* about something that interests *you*. That's how it works," snapped Poornora as she turned to go up the steps. "Tit for tat."

"You were hanging out with Poornora?" said J.J.

"This *morning*?" said Tom.

"What—did Casey say you had to or something?" asked Andrew, rolling his eyes.

"Nuh-uh . . . no . . . not exactly," I stammered. Then it was like *zap*. My mind was blank and I was out of words. I looked at the boys, who were staring up at me, their mouths open. I looked at my doughnut, but it seemed to have turned to stone.

71

Turnabout

That child kicked sand on me," said Poornora the next day when we were up at the beach. She pointed to some kid I'd never seen before and who was already about a zillion miles down the beach. "The one that's running."

Nanny sighed and said, "This is a beach, Poornora, and it's, well, sandy."

Poornora took a towel out of her bag and wrapped it around her legs, like maybe she was turning herself into a mummy. She unrolled her sleeves and pulled her floppy straw hat so far down that her face seemed to disappear up into it. "This chair isn't very steady," she said. "Tottery, maybe, and probably not good for my back."

Aunt Lois sighed and said, "We could bring a chaise up for you, if you think that would help. But like Mom said, this is the beach and it's not quite the same as—"

"I don't ever remember saying that I *liked* the beach. Besides, a chaise would just bring on that achy, tingling feeling in my extremities." Then Poornora let out the biggest-ever sigh, and without actually getting up and moving, everyone seemed to sort of inch away from her.

Including me. I mean, it's not that I make a habit of hanging out with the grownups under the umbrellas (three in a row, like we'd set up a town of our own or something), but I'd just come out of the water and was already beginning to feel totally fried and I'd ducked in to borrow a bit of shade. So I rolled across the sand, all the way over to where Lily and Liz were playing cards.

"Yeow, Ben," said Lily, unless it was Liz—I never was sure which was which. "You're getting sand on our towel."

I thought about giving them the old this-is-the-beach-and-the-beach-is-sandy routine, but instead I just rolled halfway back and lay facedown, feeling the heat of the sun on my back. I felt scritchy and scratchy all over. Then, out of the blue, I thought back to Mr. Kelly's fourth-grade class and the whole philosophy-of-life thing with the all-right and not-all-right stuff. And I was pretty sure that at that exact moment the not-all-right was taking over my life.

Eventually I pushed myself up out of the sand, just in time to see Uncle John heading across the beach toward us and carrying some kind of canvas bag. Aunt Sally was with him, waving a clipboard and a bunch of papers out in front and calling, "Okay, everybody. It's time to start the boccie tournament. I've got the schedule made out."

"What's boccie?" I said out loud, but not really *to* anybody, except that my words seemed to fall into an empty space in the conversation and I was suddenly bombarded with answers.

"It's this really cool game . . ."

". . . played right here on the beach . . ."

"Everybody gets a partner and . . ."

"We do this a lot in our family," said Casey, flopping down on the sand beside me. "Have boccie tournaments, I mean. First off, you get a partner and then you pick what color balls you want—that's because the game is played with these heavy wooden balls . . . Oh yes, and there's this small white ball and that's the one you try to get closest to." She squirted sunblock into her hand and smeared it over her arms and legs. "I'm not explaining this very well, am I?"

"Not really," I said.

"That's okay—don't worry. You'll figure it out after you watch for a few minutes." Casey turned and called to Aunt Sally, saying, "Hey, Sal—who's Ben's partner?"

Aunt Sally flipped through her stack of papers for a minute and then said, "Ben and J.J. are partners, and they're due to play at three-thirty."

"Okay," said Casey, getting up and reaching down to give me a hand. "Why don't you go track down J.J. and maybe you two can practice a bit before the tournament gets started."

But as I was heading down to the water's edge to look for J.J., Casey called me back, saying, "Oh, Ben, would you do me one quick favor before you go? Please run back to the house and ask Mitch to bring Maudie to the beach as soon as she wakes up from her nap. Tell him that the boccie tournament is about to start. It won't take you a minute."

When I got to the house, Mitch and Maudie were just starting out for the beach. Mitch was carrying Maudie, and Maudie was carrying a giant green-and-white ball and saying "Duck, duck, duck." And that's when I made my Dumb Mistake. Instead of turning around and heading right back with them, I went inside and up to the kitchen for a drink of water.

And there was Poornora, sitting on one end of the couch.

"Ah, boy," she said, "I was hoping you'd come. I figured you'd soon have enough of all that sun and sand, just as I did. Anyway, it's turnabout time."

"What's turnabout time?" I asked, between gulps of water.

"I thought I explained that to you," she said. "How I told you some of what I know about the flora and fauna of the Outer Banks—and now it's *your* turn to tell me what you know about some interesting subject."

My turn? Interesting subject? Turnabout?

"But, Poornora," I sputtered, "it's the boccie tournament and I have to find J.J. so we can practice, and besides, it's our turn to play at three-thirty and if I'm not there—"

"They'll find someone else," said Poornora.

"And not only that, but I don't really *know* anything that's even a *little* bit interesting and . . . and . . ." I stopped and drank down another whole glass of water even though I was about ready to pop. "In fact, I'll bet anything that I'm probably the most *un*interesting person you've ever met, so maybe what I should do is go back to the beach and—"

"Don't sell yourself short, Ben," said Poornora. "Now let's just think about this for a minute. What do you like to do in your spare time? Stamp collecting? Stargazing? Do you like maps or jigsaw puzzles, or could you maybe explain the rules of chess to me?"

Every time I shook my head, I felt the water sloshing around inside of me. I thought, and thought, and after a while I said, "Well, there're my *Lord of the Rings* DVDs. I guess we could watch one of those."

"What Lord? Of what Ring?" said Poornora.

"Well, it's this trilogy thing. I mean, it's three movies, only first they were books by this Tolkien guy, which I haven't actually read yet, but they, the movies, are really cool and they take place in Middle Earth and there're these good guys and bad guys and—"

"I'm not a complete fool. I do know who 'this Tolkien guy' is. Now do you know how to work this machine?" asked Poornora, pointing to the DVD player.

"I do," I said, nodding.

"Then get your DV-whatever-it-is and let's get started."

So that explains why Poornora and I spent a sunny summer afternoon sitting on opposite ends of the couch watching a movie. Which is something that would have made any other grownup in the whole entire world say "Turn that thing off and get outside."

Now I had this theory that once Poornora got into *The Fellowship of the Ring* I would sneak off and go back to the beach. Then, amazingly, I'd turn out to be this awesome boccie player and J.J. and I would win the tournament. And that I'd get back to the house just in time for the final credits and be there to whisk the DVD out of the machine.

But it didn't happen that way. That's because Poornora kept asking questions, like "Who's Frodo?" and "Who's Sam?" Then I had to stop and explain how Sam, who was incredibly brave and loyal, was this really good friend to Frodo and insisted on going along when Frodo set out on his quest. Next she wanted to know what hobbits were and why they had furry feet. After that it was about elves and dwarves and even orcs and how she was supposed to tell the difference between Saruman and Gandalf when they looked alike. And why Sauron was so evil.

And so I sat there through what should have been a perfect beach afternoon trying to explain one of my all-time-favorite movies to someone named Poornora, who wasn't even related to me. And the weird thing was that, even though I didn't want to be there, there was a deep-down part of me that liked telling her about this movie.

"You know, boy," said Poornora as I was taking the disk out of the machine, "every Frodo needs a Sam, don't you think?"

And I was just maybe going to tell her about Will back at MacCauley and the stuff we did together, when there were thumping footsteps on the stairs and J.J. came up into the living room.

"Thanks a lot," he said. "I got stuck with having Barney as my boccie partner when you didn't show up, and we lost. Big-time."

Once he said what he had to say, J.J. grabbed a bottle of water out of the fridge and thumped his way back down the steps. And I sat there feeling small and wormy.

It didn't help when Poornora let out a sort of hum and said, "It's not nice to disappoint people, boy. Not nice at all."

There was plenty I wanted to say to Poornora right then, like how I'd *told* her about the boccie tournament and that I was supposed to be there. And how *she* had said they'd find someone else. But when I looked over at her, she was busy reading the back of the DVD case, a funny, twitchy thing happening to her lips.

Family
Picture

ig-time . . . big-time . . . big-time . . . J.J.'s words kept echoing through my head. Right about then I wanted to get hold of my father and tell him he'd ruined my life, and ask if we couldn't go back to when it was just the two of us. And to remind him how at that exact moment I could be at soccer camp in West Virginia, or home alone in Baltimore, or even staying with Aunt Jo and Uncle Charlie. Instead of here—miserable—in Duck.

But mostly I needed to clue him in about how this whole family thing wasn't really so great, and that I didn't think much of being surrounded by nine thousand of Casey's relatives. I'm sure the kids were convinced I was nerd-of-the-world on account of every time they saw me I was hanging out with a whiny old lady in funny clothes, and the grownups probably thought I was a goody-goody creep.

No sooner had I thought these thoughts, though, than I got slammed with one of those not-sure feelings because, to tell the absolute honest truth, I couldn't imagine going back to a time without Casey and Maudie Mingmei. And then, to be one hundred percent fair, I thought how maybe, just maybe, Poornora couldn't help being whiny or wearing funny clothes. *But she still wasn't my problem.*

I got up and headed into the kitchen for a Sprite, zipped open the top, and stood at the back window looking down at the swimming pool. Just about everybody was out there, either in the water or sitting on the steps and around the edge. Except for Poornora, who sat facing the fence and holding a rain umbrella over her head. Mitch was in the middle of the pool, lying back on a blue floating raft with Maudie sitting on his stomach—and Casey's whole giant family spread out around him.

And right away it was like double-duh. Suddenly one of those things I'd worked hard at not thinking about bubbled to the top of my head and I wondered if, in all those years since my mother died, my father had actually been lonely. And how maybe he'd always known that somewhere out there a Casey was waiting for him. Same as Casey'd known that a little girl in China had been waiting for us.

Instead of going down to the pool, I went back into the living room and sat on the platform thing around the fireplace, next to the big wooden flamingo, and thought some more about Mitch. And myself, too. I thought about how, through the years, Mitch had never told me much about my mother, maybe on account of it made him too sad. And how—and this is where it gets a little

80

bizarre—now that we have Casey, maybe someday he'll be able to tell me more.

But one thing about my father: if he really had been lonely all those years, he'd never once let on. I mean, just the opposite. He'd made it seem like we were on this great adventure together. Just the two of us.

Another thing about Mitch was how he pretty much seemed to think I was okay the way I was. For example, there's the whole reading thing and how, even though he probably kept hoping I'd change, he never laid a guilt thing on me for not being much of a reader. Which he definitely was.

I mean, my father, who would drive clear across town to save a penny on a gallon of gas, practically fell into any bookstore he ever saw—and always bought something. And when I got hooked on my first *Lord of the Rings* movie, he went out and bought me all three books. He wasn't exactly what you'd call subtle about it because from that moment on, it was as if those books had legs and followed me around the house, forever turning up on the breakfast table or the back porch or my bedside table. No matter how many times I stuffed them back in the bookcase.

He even brought them to Duck, somehow shoving them into the car that was so full it was about ready to explode. Like I was really going to read my way through the week. Yeah, sure.

But the thing is, maybe Mitch did me a favor. Because that night, just the sight of those three books sitting on the top of my dresser gave me an idea. I'd been lying in bed thinking about Poornora and wondering how I was going to get out of spending the rest of my so-called vacation going on bird walks and watching DVDs with her. It wasn't that Nanny and Fred and the seventy thousand other relatives were *mean* to her—but every time they came up with something for her to do, Poornora always said it was too sunny, too hot, too windy, or not good for her arthritis. Then everybody went off to the beach or the pool or to play volleyball and Poornora was left sitting on her end of the couch flipping pages of a magazine.

Boring. That's when the idea hit me and I got up out of bed and went upstairs, feeling my way through the dark living room and putting my three *Lord of the Rings* books on the table right next to Poornora's place.

When I came up for breakfast the next morning, Poornora was deep into *The Fellowship of the Ring* and didn't even look up. She didn't look up when Nanny and Fred came in from their walk, or when Mitch turned on the TV to check the news, or when Casey and Maudie came up the steps singing that dumb little teapot song.

And when Tom, Matt, and Andrew arrived to say that the uncles—George, John, Tom, Jeff, and Barney—were taking the boys down to Kitty Hawk to the Wright Brothers National Memorial and did Mitch and Fred and I want to go, I figured I was home free. I mean, Poornora was glued to that book.

But Nanny had heard. "Boys?" she said. "What about the girls?"

"Girls?" said Andrew, rubbing at a spot on the rug with his bare foot. "Well . . . I guess girls could go . . . if they wanted to . . ."

"I suggest you boys go around to each of the three houses then, and see just who wants to go," said Nanny, reaching out and ruffling Andrew's hair in that way grownups have of trying to get kids to do something they don't want to do.

We never got to find out the result of the great Kitty Hawk survey, though, because at that moment Aunt Lois came up the steps saying, "I just got a call from the photographer and it's supposed to rain tomorrow, so he wants to take the family picture this afternoon."

Sounds simple, huh? I mean, everybody goes outside and stands someplace and some dude takes a picture, right? But it doesn't work that way because in Casey's family everything is a *very big deal*. Especially the family picture.

The point of the picture was that it was Nanny and Fred's fiftieth anniversary, which seemed to make it an even bigger big deal. Which may explain why within five minutes twenty-seven people were crowded into our living room—until Poornora took her book and went out onto the porch. Then there were twenty-six.

That's about when I started planning my getaway, figuring that since I really wasn't a part of this family the picture didn't concern me. The trouble was, with a bunch of uncles blocking the stairs and Poornora already on the porch, I was trapped. So I scrunched back in a corner and let the arguments swirl around me.

"We ought to have the picture taken on the beach," said Aunt Sally.

"It's sometimes windy up there," said Aunt Gloria.

"But who cares about wind?" said Casey. "We're at the shore, so the picture should be on the beach."

"Unless we had it done with all of us lined along the steps outside," put in Aunt Lois.

"Or on top of a dune—with Fred and Nanny in the middle and everybody else around them," said Uncle Tom.

"*Or,*" said Nanny, her voice suddenly louder than all the others, "we could leave it up to the photographer since he's the professional and knows about these things."

It was quiet for a minute and then everybody started nodding and saying "Uh-huh," like this was an idea that would never have occurred to them. And right away I thought that everything was settled and those of us who were interested would set off for Kitty Hawk and the Wright Brothers National Memorial.

Wrong.

Because before we could escape, Aunt Lois said, "Okay, what's everybody going to wear for the picture?"

"Wear?" said Uncle George. "Just regular clothes—whatever we have on."

"But maybe not bathing suits," put in Aunt Sally.

"Well, I've been thinking," said Aunt Lois, "that each family should pick a color and then everyone in that family would wear a T-shirt of that particular color. And that way anyone who sees the picture would know who's who."

"But who's going to see it besides us? And we already *know* who's who," called Uncle John from the far side of the room where he was reading the paper.

"I've *seen* pictures like that," said Aunt Lois, her voice suddenly snappish, "and they looked great."

"But, Lois," said Casey, "have you considered that there are six families, plus Nanny and Fred, plus Poornora—where are we going to find that many colors?"

"There's red and blue and green and yellow and purple and—"

"We're not wearing purple T-shirts," said the Liz and Lily twins. "Not in a million years."

"And even if we did pick various colors, how do we know we can find the right sizes?" asked Aunt Ellen.

And that's the way it went, round and round and round, until it ended up that everybody was supposed to wear a regular T-shirt that wasn't ragged or ratty-looking and didn't have writing on it. Which of course meant that Casey and the aunts (with us kids in tow) had to head off to the shops because no one except Maudie could come up with a T-shirt that wasn't ragged and ratty and didn't say Baltimore Orioles or Jamaica or somebody's Little League on the front.

Late in the afternoon, when it was time for the photographer to come, I hid out in my room, figuring with everything that was going on no one would notice if I wasn't there. The trouble was, I didn't take into consideration Mitch-of-the-Eagle-Eye. I mean, there I was lying on my bed, staring at the ceiling and imagining it covered with a detailed map of Middle Earth, when my father knocked, then burst through the door.

"Ben, come on. Everybody's waiting. It's picture time," he said as he propelled me out the side door. When we got around front, there was Aunt Sally urging Poornora along and saying, "Don't be silly—of course you're a part of this family." And with that, Poornora looked straight at me and did something with one eye that maybe was and maybe wasn't a wink.

Down on the beach a photographer named Luke was arranging and rearranging people, shuffling them like a deck of cards. When he saw Poornora and me, I was sure he was going to lose it—but he just stood for a minute, raking his fingers through his hair and looking up at the sky. Then, with a wave of his hand, he pointed to a spot at one end of the front row and said, "You two—there."

"With my arthritis? You want me down there? Don't any of you people know that this could lead to sciatica, or maybe lumbago?" I heard Poornora muttering as Aunt Lois and Casey helped her onto the sand. When she was settled, with a beach towel draped over her legs, I sat beside her, leaning as far in the other direction as I could without falling over.

"If I thought I could get up again, then the two of us could sneak around the edge of the group and disappear," Poornora whispered in my direction. "And they'd never know we were gone."

And the weird thing was that I suddenly found myself whispering back, "Maybe you could slither, sort of like a snake, and we could just inch away."

I was sitting there trying to decide if Poornora and I really could manage our big escape when, at the other end of the group, Maudie wiggled out of Casey's arms and ran toward us. She spun around once before plunking herself down between the two of us.

"Cheese, everyone," Luke the photographer called.

The camera clicked.

And there we were—me, Poornora, and Maudie Mingmei together in the family picture.

Borrrrrrring

When I went to bed that night, I was sure that to-morrow would be the best Duck-day ever. I mean, by now Poornora was totally into the *Lord of the Rings* books and I could look forward to a whole day with nothing to do but hang out at the beach.

But just as Luke the photographer had predicted, the next day it rained. And rained. And rained. All day long, starting in the morning way before any of us were awake. It rained so much that the towels in the bathroom felt damp and clammy and when I went to read the comics, the newspaper sort of folded over like a wet noodle.

For some reason, no one seemed to think this was a very good day for going to the Wright Brothers National Memorial. In fact, no one seemed to think it was a good day for doing much of *anything*.

Fred settled down to watch CNN. Poornora kept reading. And after a bunch of phone calls back and forth, Casey, Nanny, and the aunts went off shopping at some place called Scarborough Faire. That left Mitch in charge of Maudie, which meant he then roped me into singing "The Itsy Bitsy Spider" and "Hickory Dickory Dock" a zillion times, with Maudie putting in an occasional " 'pider" or "mouse."

After lunch, Maudie took a nap, and so did my father and Fred. Poornora went right on reading except that from time to time she looked up and said, "This much rain isn't a good sign. It probably means a hurricane's coming and the whole crowd of us are going to have to evacuate. You mark my word, boy." That's when I cut a hole in the bottom of a giant trash bag, turning it into a poncho, and headed out to find something to do.

First I went across the street to house number three looking for J.J., thinking maybe I could say something about the boccie tournament and how I was sorry for not showing up. And how, after that, he might suggest that the two of us go up to the beach and videotape the storm. But Uncle Barney answered the door and said, "Oh, sorry, Ben, but J.J.'s dad took him to Corolla to spend the afternoon with some friends he knows from home." Then he asked if I wanted to come in anyway and help Sophie and Sara make chocolate chip cookies.

I didn't, and kept on down the street to house number two, where Liz and Lily were sitting on the porch. They were each holding a CD player and wearing earphones, and it was like I could hear music oozing out of their heads. "I'm looking for the boys," I shouted.

"Not home," said Lily (or Liz). "Nobody's home but us."

"They all went down to Kill Devil Hill," said the other one, "to visit some cousins on Aunt Sally's side of the family."

"Thanks," I said as I headed back up the street, wondering how come everybody seemed to have friends on the Outer Banks while just about all the people I knew in the whole world were at soccer camp in West Virginia.

When I got to the volleyball court, I found the twins Barney and Bobby sloshing from one sandy, gritty hole to the next and chasing each other with butterfly nets. I watched them for a while before moving on up to the beach. Once there I stood, half hypnotized, staring at the giant waves and feeling the way the whole world seemed to shake as they pounded onto the shore. The wind howled and bits of sand stung my face, so I shook myself like a big wet dog and went back to the house, where I settled onto the first-floor porch. I sat *there* for I-don't-know-how-long, the rain dripping through the upstairs porch and making crackly noises on my garbage-bag poncho.

Borrrrrrring.

Eventually I gave up the whole outdoor thing and went inside, figuring I'd look at one of my *Lord of the Rings* movies—maybe *The Return of the King*, because that's my favorite—to sort of save the day. But by then Fred was up from his nap and back watching CNN.

Which pretty much sums up one (boring) (rainy) day of my vacation.

Except that that night we went out for pizza, which should have been great, but wasn't. Not the pizza part, but the going out.

It started when, late in the afternoon, Mitch knocked on my bedroom door and came in, saying, "Hey, Ben, I looked for you a while ago—thought maybe we could play cards or something—but you'd disappeared. Where'd you get to?"

I shrugged, thinking back on my not-so-thrilling afternoon. "Nowhere. Just around, I guess. I mean, what's there *to do* in the rain?"

"I'm sorry about that—the weather really didn't cooperate today, did it? But come on, we're heading out the road for pizza—you, Casey, Maudie, and me—so be upstairs at six. Okay?"

"Just us?" I asked.

"Just us," my father said.

Good, I thought, as I peeled off my dirty T-shirt and replaced it with a not-so-dirty one. *Definitely good.*

But I should have known that in Casey's monster family there was no such thing as *just us*. By the time we got out front, Aunt Lois, Uncle Barney, Sophie, Sara, Bobby, and Barney were waiting for us.

"Shall we walk or ride?" asked Aunt Lois. "The rain's stopped and the sky's starting to clear."

"Walking's fine, right?" said Casey, nodding vaguely at Mitch and me.

I looked at my father and he looked at me; then he gave one of those "What're you going to do?" shrugs as he hoisted Maudie into her stroller and we all started down the street. Just as we were passing house number three, J.J. and Uncle Jeff came down off the porch.

"We'll walk with you guys," said Uncle Jeff. "Ellen's helping Ellie look for her flip-flops, and they'll be along in a minute."

So the *just us* crowd trailed the rest of the way down Sea Hawk Drive and turned onto Route 12, with J.J. and me bringing up the rear. We walked along, kicking at stones and not talking till J.J. said, "You know something—about the boccie tournament. It didn't really matter, 'cause the grownups always win."

"Yeah, I'm sure," I said. "Except I should've been there."

"Well, okay, but . . ." J.J. shrugged, then kicked his stone extra hard so that it shot off the path and disappeared into the pine needles. "Did you want to come?"

"To get pizza? Yeah, I guess. Why not?"

"No, not the pizza," said J.J. "To Duck. Did you want to come to Duck?"

"Not really," I said. "You see, there was this soccer camp."

"In West Virginia?" said J.J., turning to look at me, his mouth gaping open.

"Yeah, in West Virginia. Why? Did you want to go there, too?"

"You know it. But then there was this whole family thing, and it being Nanny and Fred's anniversary. And the best my dad could come up with was 'Maybe next year.'"

"Fathers say that a lot," I said. "That and 'We'll see.'"

"And 'Some other time,'" said J.J. as we raced to catch up with the rest of the group.

The pizza place was steamy, noisy, and super crowded, but we finally got a long picnic table in the back, under a ceiling fan that went *svish svish svish* as it swung around. Mostly then I just buried myself in pizza, which was hot and cheesy and loaded with pepperoni—the way I liked it. After we were done, J.J. and I went out on the deck and stood dropping bits of gravel into the sound while we waited for the rest of them.

"Tomorrow's crabbing day," said J.J. "The dads are taking the kids, early, at seven o'clock. At least they say they are—if there's not too much other stuff to be done. Anyway, you in?"

"Yeah," I said. "Crabbing sounds good. Really good."

The
Buzz

Crabbing didn't happen either.

Not because it was raining—which it wasn't. Not because we'd all overslept—which we hadn't. And certainly not because us kids had things we'd rather do—which we didn't. In fact, there we were, Tom, Matt, Andrew, J.J., Sophie, Sara, Barney, Bobby, and me, bunched outside of house number one, talking about how many crabs we were going to catch and how big they'd be, and which one of us would get the most.

Later on, once it was obvious we really weren't going anywhere, I thought back to the night before and how J.J. had said that the dads were taking the kids up to a place on the sound to go crabbing "if there's not too much other stuff to be done." The trouble was, I hadn't paid enough attention to that part of the sentence and apparently there was *other stuff to be done*. A ton of it.

I should have known, because as soon as I woke up I could sense the sort of buzz that was filling the house, pushing through open windows and doors, and then reaching out to the other two houses, like an electric current.

The aunts and Casey ran from house to house, calling out things like "Mum's the word" and "Hush-hush," and "A big surprise" as they passed us kids on the volleyball court, where we'd hunkered down, waiting for something to happen. The uncles and Mitch were sent on errands and came back to unload mysterious bags and boxes at house number three before heading out again.

After a while, the other kids started drifting off. First Tom and Matt and Andrew, then Sophie and Sara, followed almost right away by Barney and Bobby, till it was just J.J. and me—still waiting for something to happen.

"Let's head over to Aunt Lois's house," said J.J., getting up and kicking at a tuft of grass before starting across the street. "That's where the action is."

"Action for what?" I asked, trailing after him. "What's going on?"

With that J.J. spun around, his shoes scritching against the sand on the street. "The party—the party," he said, yanking me out of the way as a trash truck rumbled down the street. "For Nanny and Fred, for their anniversary. That's what the whole week's about—their fiftieth."

"Yeah, but I thought after the family picture that was it," I said.

"Wrong," said J.J. "Tonight's the big deal. Tonight's the party."

"And it's supposed to be a *surprise*? And you guys don't think that with everything that's going on your grandparents haven't figured it out?" I said.

"You didn't," answered J.J., grinning and giving me his best you-really-are-a-dim-bulb look. "Nanny and Fred are probably sharper than you are, but even if they did figure it out, they wouldn't let on because they're cool about stuff like that. Now come on." And he led the way up the steps of house number three.

Inside, the electric-current feeling was even stronger and the house seemed to vibrate. Lily and Liz were busy stringing crepe-paper streamers around the living room, crisscrossing reds and greens and yellows. In the kitchen, Aunts Gloria and Ellen were dicing and stirring while Aunt Lois sat at the breakfast bar folding paper napkins and calling out orders.

"Uh-oh," said J.J., stopping at the top of the steps and nudging me to back up the way we'd come. "Looks like big-time work over here. Head for the door."

"Why don't we just go to the beach?" I said as we went across the street.

"Grownups are busy. Nobody to watch us. And the only way we could do it was if we didn't go in the water, and that'd freak me out on a great beach day like this."

"How about the lifeguard?"

"No lifeguard," said J.J. "In case you hadn't noticed—it's an unguarded beach."

"How about Nanny and Fred, then?"

"Too old," said J.J. "Well, they're not really old-old, but they both say they're too old to watch us kids in the ocean. I guess in case they had to rush in and rescue someone. But come on. Let's check out your place."

Which was definitely a mistake. I mean, we just walked in the door and there was Casey, waiting for me. "Ben, thank heavens. Mitch is out running errands, and I've been hoping you'd turn up because I desperately need you to watch Maudie for a bit while I go help across the street. Okay? It's such a pretty day—maybe a walk, but keep her away from the beach. And if you really get desperate, she could watch one short little video. I made her lunch and it's in the fridge. If I'm not back by naptime—well, you know the drill. I really, really appreciate it." With that, Casey was gone. And, after a quick "See ya," so was J.J.

Up in the living room, Maudie and I sang "The Itsy Bitsy Spider" maybe forever. Then I sang that little teapot song for an eternity, with her doing the handle and the spout thing. We were just starting in on it again when Poornora, who had taken up her place on the porch with her floppy beach hat and her rain umbrella and her book, got up and called through the screen door. "Boy, boy, doesn't that child know any other songs?"

"I guess," I said, sighing. "She likes 'Hickory Dickory Dock.' "

"Mouse," called Maudie as I started to sing.

It was just after twelve when Fred and Nanny came

back from the beach and Poornora came in from the porch, and in a weird and not-so-weird way the five of us sat at the table and ate lunch together. Which was actually the highlight of my day up to that point.

"It's beautiful at the beach—I can't imagine why the rest of them weren't up there this morning," said Nanny in that fake wide-eyed voice that grownups sometimes use.

"Yeah, well, I don't know," I mumbled.

"Hmmmmph," said Poornora.

"Mouse," shouted Maudie.

Once I'd gotten Maudie Mingmei settled for her nap, I went back upstairs. Poornora had moved inside (still with the hat, but she'd ditched the umbrella) and settled on the end of the big couch. "Ho, boy, desperate times call for desperate measures," she said, pointing to the other couch where she'd propped my copy of *The Fellowship of the Ring* against a pillow. "I've finished with that one and I thought you might want to start. There doesn't seem to be anything else to do."

I groaned on the inside as I flopped down on the couch, picked up the book, and looked at it like it was some kind of alien object. Then, almost without meaning to, I opened it and started to read, dragging my eyes over the words and reluctantly turning the pages. Slowly at first, then faster, and even faster.

• • •

Later in the afternoon, when Casey and Mitch had come home and were back in charge of Maudie, and when the electric-current buzz in the house had settled into a kind of hum, I sat on a wobbly rocker under the porch, staring up at the row of bathing suits hanging on the line. I wasn't thinking of the bathing suits, though, but about how, nothing against Nanny and Fred, I really one hundred percent didn't want to go to their party tonight. How I wished maybe I could disappear. For a while, anyway.

"You could. *We* could," said Poornora, as she came around the side of the house.

"Could what?" I said.

"Disappear."

I lurched, the chair wobbled, and I had to catch myself to keep from landing on the ground. "Did I say that out loud?" I croaked. "Did I?"

"Great minds, boy. Great minds," said Poornora. "You didn't *say* it, but it's been on your face all day, just as I suspect it's been on mine. And we could, you know. Disappear."

"How?" I asked.

"Drift off, go someplace, for a bit anyway. Do you really think they'd notice if we weren't here for the Big Bash?"

"They wouldn't miss me," I said. "But they'd miss you, for sure."

"Piffle," said Poornora, moving over to straighten a sea-horse towel on the line. "Double piffle."

"Where?" I said. "I mean, where would we go?"

"Well," said Poornora as she worked her way along the line, rehanging the bathing suits and fastening each with a clothespin she took from a yellow basket, "I've given it some thought, and there's a place called Scarborough Faire I've heard them all talk about. Down this street, then right on the main one and up a ways."

"What is it, though?"

"A little of this and a bit of that," Poornora said. "A place to shop, to eat. Books, kites, peanuts, and, I suspect, the ever-present T-shirt. And, it is devoutly to be wished, a place to get an ice cream cone on an August afternoon. Are you ready?"

I stared at Poornora in her floppy hat and her droopy shorts and her shirt made of some slimy kind of cloth, at the purse hanging on her arm and even the plastic rain bonnet dangling from her pocket, and knew that she was positively not kidding. That, more than anything, this Poornora—the new one—wanted a giant ice cream cone. And that we were going to Scarborough Faire to get it.

"Are you ready?" she asked again.

"Soon's I go get my shoes and some money," I said, hesitating, half expecting her, at any minute, to call out "Joke!" or "Gotcha!" "But what happens if they see us walking down the street? What then?"

"Nature walk, boy. Nature walk," Poornora said.

"It's important to check the flora and the fauna, don't you agree? Now move along."

"Yeah, well, okay. But one thing, Poornora. And it's important. My name is *Ben*."

"Picky, picky," Poornora said, taking her rain bonnet out, smoothing it, and putting it back in her pocket. "What's in a name, boy? What's in a name?"

"But—"

"Don't you think I know where they got *my* name? But the way I see it, Nora sounds harsh, while Poornora fairly *rolls* off the tongue. So—what's in a name?"

"Yeah, but—my name is Ben."

"Ben, then," said Poornora, with a nod. "Ben."

Poornora and I made it to the end of Sea Hawk Drive without anyone paying much attention, like maybe we really were invisible. I mean, a woman walking a yellow lab said it was a nice day for a walk, wasn't it, and Lily (or Liz) waved from a porch, and Uncle Tom tooted his horn as he pulled into the driveway of house number two. But no one asked where we were going, or when we'd be back, or told us not to be late for the party.

We got to the corner and turned right, starting up a sort of hill, and the farther we went, the slower Poornora walked. When we found a bench in a shady spot, we sat down and I pretended that I was really into watching the joggers and people on bikes who kept zooming past. Once Poornora stopped making those huffing sounds when she breathed, she stood up and said, "Well, Ben, shall we forge ahead? Onward. Upward."

Since Route 12 is the only up-and-down street in Duck, it was choked with cars. Poornora and I stuck to the bike lane, making way for people coming the other way and dodging cyclists who came along behind us, calling "On the left." We made our way past restaurants and gas stations and shops set back from the street until finally, just as Poornora was beginning to huff and puff again, I saw a sign up ahead.

"Look. Scarborough Faire. We're almost there," I called.

Scarborough Faire

'm not sure how to describe Scarborough Faire. I mean, it wasn't a mall, all glitzy, with escalators and music and a gazillion stores. But it was definitely about shopping and looked like a bunch of beach cottages strung together with a big long porch wrapping around a lot of it. The porch itself was lined with benches that were pretty much filled with men checking their watches and tapping their feet while they waited for their wives, or girlfriends, or sisters, or daughters.

"Ah, me," said Poornora, settling into an empty space on a bench in front of a T-shirt shop. "I'll rest a bit while you check things out—not far, mind you, because I'll be up and ready to go any minute now."

I drifted off, looking in windows at shirts and flip-flops and things made of shells, skipping the jewelry shop and parking myself in front of the kite place. I peered in at dragons and caterpillars and kites that looked like giant bats, only red and green and purple. I inched closer to the door, ready to slip inside, hoping that Poornora was maybe looking the other way.

"Ben, Ben, not too far, boy, I want us to get going to-gether."

I froze, half in and half out the door, willing the floor to open up and swallow me. Which it didn't. I was posi-tive that everybody on the Outer Banks, maybe even in all of North Carolina, was staring at me, their eyeballs mak-ing pinpricks on my back.

"Ben, yoo-hooooooo," Poornora called, stretching out the *hooooooo* so that it seemed to go on forever.

"I think your grandmother's calling you," said a woman in a crab T-shirt, tapping me on the shoulder.

"Oh, okay, I guess," I said, inching my way around. "But she's not my grandmother."

Poornora had her hat off and was waving it in big cir-cular swoops, still calling "Yoo-hooooooo." For a minute I thought my arm had turned to lead, that it was super-glued to the side of my body and wouldn't move. But the crab-woman was still looking at me and I finally dragged it up, swinging it back and forth as I started along the porch toward Poornora.

What I really wanted to do was to run in the opposite direction. To leap over the railing and head for the park-ing lot, or disappear into a shop and lose myself in the racks of beach cover-ups and sweatshirts hanging there. To never have come to Duck in the first place.

When I got to where Poornora was sitting, she gave me some kind of long-lost-relative smile, then turned to the man sitting next to her and said, "Here he is. I knew he wouldn't have gone far—he's a good boy."

Yikes. My face burned and I swallowed hard. I mean, here was Poornora telling some stranger how good I was when all I'd wanted to do was to run away. To pretend I didn't know her with her yoo-hoos and her funny clothes.

"I'm here," I said, moving to stand beside her. "Where shall we go?"

"That way," she said, planting her hat back on her head and getting up. "The gentleman I was talking to said there's a decoy shop along the way and, beyond that, a bookstore and a kitchen place. There's another building across the way, and we still need to find our ice cream cones." And with that, Poornora took off, like the Little Engine That Could, chugging along the porch and down the path, past the gazebo, with me trailing along behind.

We went in and out of shops, looking at aprons with dumb sayings across the front, and at crab mallets and salt and pepper shakers in the shape of lighthouses. In just about every store, Poornora kept up a running commentary, announcing in a too-loud voice exactly what was wrong with everything we saw.

After a while, we climbed the stairs and headed into the decoy store, a place crammed with all kinds of neat stuff like ducks and gulls and sandpipers carved out of wood. No sooner had the screen door slapped shut behind us than Poornora stood up way tall and breathed in the musty woody smell. "Ah," she said, softly. "I feel at home here."

In the beginning she scurried around, pointing out loons and mallards and teals to me, running her fingers along painted feathers. Then she spotted a rooster—sort of a faded white one with a yellow beak and red comb. It was perched on a green ball in a top-of-the-world sort of pose and looked set to crow at any minute.

"This is a good example of folk art," she said, picking it up and moving it to another shelf, then standing back to look at it some more. She did that a bunch of times, moving the rooster from shelf to tabletop to windowsill, all the while making humming noises in her throat.

"Why don't you buy it?" I asked, thinking maybe that was the only way I'd get her out of here. "I mean, I'll carry it back to the house for you."

"Hmmmmm," Poornora hummed again. "I could— but I don't think so. You know something, Ben? The thing about these places is they make you realize how many things you don't need."

"Yeah, but if you want it . . . why not?"

Poornora seemed to think for a minute, then she shook her head. "I know he's here, sitting on that windowsill—which is much the better place for him, don't you think? And any time I need him, I can just close my eyes and there he'll be. Waiting."

I looked at her to see if she was for real. I wanted to ask what planet she was from. But instead, I blinked a bunch of times and said, "Yeah, but the thing is—I like *having* my bike a lot better than just closing my eyes and knowing it's in a store someplace. And my skateboard, too."

"Point taken, Ben. And I agree, bikes and skateboards are notable exceptions," said Poornora. "Now come along."

We spent a lot of time in the bookstore, but I guess Poornora thought she could just close her eyes and *see* the books, too, because she didn't buy anything there either. After that, we went to a sort-of-everything shop and Poornora stood in the doorway, looking over the scene and announcing in a rattly kind of voice, "Nonsense. Pure nonsense, Ben-boy. Who could possibly need any of this?"

She sorted through refrigerator magnets and key chains before moving to a counter at the back of the store where she began to try on sunglasses. They were just regular ones to start, but then they got funkier and funkier. Finally Poornora swung around, a pair of glasses with sticking-out eyelashes across the top and a zigzag of beads along the sides perched on her nose. "Well, Ben, tell me what you think. Now you try a pair."

Suddenly there was a sort of echo from three guys over by the magazine rack, calling out in warbly, fake Poornora voices, "Yeah, Ben, *tell her what you think.* Go ahead, *now you try a pair.*"

I totally froze and, more than anything, I wanted Poornora to disappear. But then I looked over at the boys and, weirder than weird, I suddenly wanted *them* to disappear even more. That's when I reached for the glasses Poornora held out to me and put them on. And through the brown-gray lenses I stared at the three of them until they turned and left the store.

And weirdest of all, after the tons of talk about things we didn't need, Poornora bought me an OBX T-shirt, the kind I didn't even know *she* knew I'd been looking at as we went from store to store. OBX means Outer Banks, and you see it a bunch of places, like on shirts and stickers people put on cars.

We found the ice cream store in the other building, across the way, close to the nut shop. There were balloons bunched outside, tied to the sign, and strips of crepe paper dangling from the ceiling. While we stood in line waiting for our cones, I all of a sudden remembered Liz and Lily stringing crepe paper that morning and wondered what was happening now, back on Sea Hawk Drive.

"What do you think they're doing—all of them?" I asked once we had settled onto a bench outside to eat our ice cream.

"Still getting ready," said Poornora, without even having to ask what *they* I was talking about. "You know, Ben, the getting ready always takes longer than what you're getting ready for."

"I guess," I said, licking around the outside edge of my cone and thinking about Casey and the aunts and how they'd been doing stuff all day. And how Mitch and the uncles had been on errand duty, and how Fred and Nanny had kept going back and forth to the beach and never once letting on they knew what was going to happen. And about the sort of buzz all through the three houses.

"Do you think maybe . . . I mean, should we go back?" I asked.

"We could," said Poornora, popping the pointy end of the cone into her mouth. "They're not apt to know we're missing, so even if we're a little late, like as not, we could just slip in." She wiped her mouth with a paper napkin, which she then folded into smaller and smaller squares and put in her purse. "But it's a long walk, Ben. And right now I need to rest."

With that, Poornora tilted her head forward, resting her chin on her chest, and closed her eyes.

The Call

And Poornora slept. Right there on the porch outside the ice cream shop with people milling around and balloons jerking in the breeze and a kid in a Lion King T-shirt pitching a fit on the next bench down.

She didn't just sleep, she slept noisily, making snorty huffing sounds that went from high to low, then back up the scale again. And sometimes a spit bubble would form on her lower lip and balance there for a while before rolling down her chin and onto her flowered blouse.

And there I was, frozen on the other end of the bench. Part of me felt like all those people in North Carolina were staring at me again, while the other part felt one hundred percent totally alone. After a bit, I got up, pacing back and forth and around Poornora's bench and trying to figure out what to do. I mean, if I woke her and she was still really tired, then no way could she walk back to the house. But if I didn't wake her, judging by the snorty huffing sounds, she could maybe go on sleeping until tomorrow.

I looked around for a phone booth, but there wasn't

one. I wished I had a cell phone, but I didn't. I wondered if there were taxis in Duck, but I couldn't leave Poornora while I hunted for one. I thumped down on the bench again, flopping against the backrest and rattling my OBX T-shirt bag in hopes she'd wake up. No luck.

I sat there trying not to panic and, at the same time, trying to figure out what to do. The panic part was definitely winning when I noticed a teenage girl with sparkly studs lined up her ear. She was leaning on a wall, talking on a cell phone, and suddenly, like a giant sunflower, a plan started to grow.

I waited for that nanosecond between when the girl ended one call and got into the next, and I jumped up and went over to her.

"Hey, I know you don't know me—and I don't know you . . . I mean, I don't know anybody here—but this thing has happened." I jerked my head in Poornora's direction. "This person I'm with—well, I guess she's like my great-aunt—she fell asleep and she's kind of old—or she *acts* kind of old—and now I think I need someone to come pick her up on account of it's a sort of long walk home. So could I please use your cell for a minute?"

"Sure," the girl said, tossing me the phone. "Do you know the number where you're staying?"

Panic time. Because, of course, I didn't. Pictures raced through my head—the shops closing for the day, everybody going home, and Poornora and me stranded forever.

"You know anybody's cell number?" the girl asked. "Your mom? Your dad?"

"Yeah, my dad. And Casey's, too."

"So call, okay?"

I called Mitch's number, but nothing happened. I called Casey's and a man with a rumbly deep voice answered.

"Hi, it's me. Ben," I said. "I need to . . . I mean, is my dad there? Or Casey?"

"I wondered who this phone belonged to," the man said. "It was on the counter, and when it rang I just picked it up. This is Fred, by the way, and Casey just ran across the street for a minute, but I'll hunt down Mitch if you need him. But, Ben, where are you? We were beginning to worry."

"At Scarborough Faire," I said.

"With Poornora?"

"Yes, sir. That's—"

"Is everything all right?" Fred wanted to know.

"Yeah, it is, except that now Poornora's asleep on a bench and I think she's really, really tired and I don't know whether she's going to be able to walk the whole way home."

"Not to worry," said Fred. "I've been looking for something useful to do all day and I'll be there ASAP. Now tell me exactly where you are, okay?"

I thought probably I should urge him not to come, even ruin the surprise and tell him that he had a party to go to at almost any minute, but instead the words spilled out as I told him about the ice cream shop with the balloons and the bench in front. And that Poornora and I would be waiting.

"Thanks a lot," I said, handing the phone back to the girl. "Someone's coming. I'm Ben, by the way."

"Cool," she said. "And I'm Ryan. See ya."

I settled down on the bench to wait for Fred, counting backward from one thousand to make the time pass. Except I kept losing my place and having to start over, so I finally gave up. Then I played some kind of dumb alphabet game, trying to find objects in sight that started with each letter but I got hung up on Q and then X, so I quit that, too.

I felt like I'd been sitting there for eons and was beginning to think maybe there was another ice cream store someplace—and that Fred was waiting for us there. Just then, though, I looked and at the far end of the porch saw Casey heading in my direction, and J.J. coming along behind. I jumped up and ran toward them, not even caring how dorky I looked.

"Casey! What . . . I mean, I thought . . . Fred said he was coming. And J.J., how come . . . ?"

"He was. Fred, I mean," said Casey, throwing her arms around my neck in a sort of stranglehold. "In fact, he was in the car ready to leave when I got home, but when he told me about your call, I knew I wanted to be the one to get you. So we traded places, and then J.J. said he'd like to come, too. But anyway, are you okay? Is Poornora?"

"Yeah, we walked up here and did a bunch of stuff, and then we had ice cream and afterward she got really tired and fell asleep," I said, pointing to Poornora's bench. "I guess we shouldn't've . . . I mean, with everything that was going on, we didn't think anybody'd notice."

"Oh, several people said they saw you and Poornora heading down Sea Hawk, and we just thought you were going for a walk. But after a while we started to worry." Casey turned away for a minute, then back to me. "I don't blame you for wanting to get away. It is overwhelming, isn't it? This whole family thing, especially for you and Poornora. There're so *many* of us, and we all tend to talk a lot, and at the same time."

"Yeah, but—"

"You know, Ben, there are times when I want to escape, too—and all these people are related to me. Like when my sister Lois gets too bossy or when I'm tired of Tom's magic tricks or Sally asks too many questions. That's the way it is with families."

The whole time she was talking, J.J. just stood there nodding his head like some kind of bobblehead doll.

"Really? You're sure?" I croaked.

"Positive," said Casey. "And besides, you've had a sort of double whammy here. I do know that, and I'm sorry. First you get me moving in, and then Maudie comes along, and now here we are on vacation with what must seem like the whole world. When you'd rather be at soccer camp. Or maybe just hanging out with your dad."

With that, J.J.'s head seemed to go at super-bobble-speed.

"Well, yeah, but . . ." And I stopped, my words just hanging there. Here was Casey saying all the stuff I'd been thinking, all the stuff I'd been so sure about, and now all of a sudden I wasn't so sure anymore. I mean, Casey and Maudie were okay. More than okay. And so were Nanny and Fred. The aunts and uncles, too, and the cousins, and I guess Poornora. And even J.J. standing there was definitely okay. But no way could I turn into a total wuss and say any of that.

We might have just kept standing there, me trying to think of a nothing kind of remark, and Casey looking at me with that sort of soft, melty look she uses mostly for Maudie Mingmei. But over on the bench, Poornora opened her eyes and straightened up. She took her hat off, then put it on again. She wiped her mouth and blinked a bunch of times.

"Casey?" she said. "Is that you? And J.J.? I must have dozed off for a second. What are you doing here?"

"Just thought we'd come by and give you guys a ride home," said Casey, going over to Poornora. "If you're ready though, let's be on our way. After all, we have a party to go to."

Casey held her hand out to Poornora, helping her off

the bench and sort of steering her along, with J.J. and me bringing up the rear. Together we made a kind of mini-parade as we went past the nut shop and the ice cream store and that girl Ryan, who was still leaning on the wall and talking on her cell phone.

"You know something?" said J.J. as we started down the steps to the parking area. "At this party tonight I have to go around and video stuff and ask questions and all and—you want to help?"

"Yeah, okay," I said. "I could do that."

The Bash

I have to say right off that the big anniversary bash was a lot like the dinner we had the first night in Duck, and a lot like some of the in-between dinners we'd had along the way. I mean, the same people were there, only a little better dressed. Not fancy or anything, but in shorts that had been ironed and shirts with the wrinkles smoothed out. And Casey and the aunts wore lipstick, which they usually didn't do.

Even though we were in house number three, Uncle John was still trying to fly his kite from off the second-floor porch, and Tom, Matt, and Andrew were still running outside to rescue it. Uncle Tom did the same magic tricks he'd been doing every day, and Sophie, Sara, and Ellie brought the Twister game. And again, Nanny sent them into another room to play.

There wasn't any popcorn, but Nanny and Fred's dog, Pongo, ate the last four spinach balls on the tray. He didn't throw up, though, so maybe dogs like spinach better than popcorn. And right on cue, Bobby spilled his root beer on the rug, and Barney stepped in it.

Nothing against the lasagna we had before, but the food at the anniversary party was definitely better. It was all seafood stuff: shrimp salad, crab cakes, and fish cooked on the grill. Besides that, there was a ton of pasta salad and potato salad and regular salad, deviled eggs, really good bread, and about a hundred kinds of pickles. Only this time, after I got my plate, I didn't stand there like nerd-of-the-world. I just looked at J.J. and he looked at me and jerked his head in the direction of the porch and said, "C'mon—the other guys are outside."

When I finished eating and had polished off my fourth deviled egg, I pushed back a little (you can't go far at a picnic table) and thought about how maybe this is what families do—a lot of the same things over and over. And how if someone new comes along (like me, and Poornora, and, I guess, Maudie Mingmei), they all just scrunch over and make room for them. And how, if anything ever happened—if one of them died, like my mother, Sara Jane, had, or even the grandparents I'd never known—then they'd all just move closer together. And how it was always like that—in and out, in and out.

I remembered that earlier in the week I'd picked up a big white photo album with *Our Wedding* on the front, and it was filled with pictures of Nanny and Fred's wedding. They looked different—skinnier and tons younger, and Fred had sticking-up hair. But in a way they looked the same as now. I thought about how back then there was just the two of them, and now there was this great huge crowd.

Luckily, before I could get all soppy thinking that stuff, J.J. poked me and said, "Cake in the living room."

Aunt Lois and Uncle Tom brought in what had to be the biggest cake I'd ever seen, and suddenly everybody was going on about how beautiful it was and how it'd come from some inn up the road and that the flowers on the top were real.

Maudie moved up close to the table, shouting "Cake, cake, cake!" Nanny cut the first piece, then handed the knife to Aunt Sally, who kept going, serving gigantic slices to every one of us.

"Hey, J.J.," said Aunt Ellen once we were done, "don't forget you're supposed to be videotaping this event. You and Ben."

After that we went around the room, asking people for comments about Nanny and Fred, or about the party, or anything they wanted to say. Here's some of the stuff we got:

"Congratulations . . ."

"You're the best . . ."

"Terrific party . . ."

"Are there seconds on the cake? . . ."

"And there hasn't even been a hurricane—yet . . ." (This from Poornora.)

Then J.J. swung the camcorder in my direction. "Your

turn," he called. "We need to know what you think." And the room suddenly got quiet.

I looked around, remembering my old philosophy of life from way back in fourth grade, and I thought that now—at this very moment—there was a ton more all-right stuff than not-all-right in my life. Like Mitch and Casey and Maudie and me, sort of lumped together. And then I thought about the extra people I'd met in the last year and a half, and how Casey's relatives were now my relatives, which actually made me a part of her monster family. And how there was one full day of vacation left, plus Saturday morning, and that maybe someday we could even come back to Duck.

J.J. cleared his throat a bunch of times and whispered, "C'mon—say something."

Mitch was across the room holding Maudie but watching me, a giant grin spread over his face. Casey gave me a thumbs-up, and Poornora nodded.

"Yeah, right, cool," I said. "I'm glad I came."

"Me too," said J.J. "Me too."

Then everybody started talking again, and the party went on.